SNOW BLIND

MVFOL

D1177047

CATHERINE FARNES

JOURNEY FORTH™

Greenville, SC 29614

Library of Congress Cataloging-in-Publication Data
Farnes, Catherine, 1964-
  Snowblind / by Catherine Farnes.
    p. cm.
  Summary: Jacy and Dakota Craig are shocked at their father's plan
to sell the family outfitting business to a wealthy guest, but a health
crisis and a snowmobile accident force the family to focus on God's
plan for their lives.
  ISBN 1-59166-329-6 (perfect bound pbk. : alk. paper)
  [1. Family life—Montana—Fiction. 2. Christian life—Fiction. 3. Win
ter sports—Fiction 4. Business enterprises—Fiction. 5. Hospitality—
Fiction. 6. Montana—Fiction.] I. Title.
  PZ7.F238265Sno 2004
  [Fic]—dc22

                                                        2004027625

Snowblind

Cover and Design by TJ Getz
© 2005 Index Stock Imagery, Inc.
Composition by Melissa Matos

© 2005 BJU Press
Greenville, SC 29614

ISBN 1-59166-329-6

15   14   13   12   11   10   9   8   7   6   5   4   3   2   1

For Mom and Georges,
for the difference you've made
in the difference we'll make.

Books by Catherine Farnes

The Rivers of Judah Series
    Rivers of Judah
    Snow
    Out of Hiding
    The Way of Escape

Over the Divide
The Slide
Snowblind

Contents

I dug into my steak like a kid in a race to find a ten-dollar bill. Not so much because I was hungry, but because I was bored. My older sister Jacy and I had been sitting at a table in the otherwise empty café for nearly an hour with Back Trails' newest client's kids, Cullen and Amberlee Wheatley. Dad had suggested shortly after the Wheatleys had pulled in that Jacy and I take them to Cooke City for dinner since we were all about the same age.

"It's not often you two get to hang around with other teen-agers in the middle of winter," he'd said.

True enough. In the busy summer tourist season, teenagers came to Back Trails all the time with their parents or with their church youth group or a high school group to hike across the East Rosebud backpacking trail or to ride ATVs on the old mining roads behind town or to fish the high mountain lakes.

But it was February now, and while Dad's outfitting business in the remote high mountains of south-central Montana attracted plenty of customers for winter camping and snowmobiling, they were mainly men traveling alone or with a couple of buddies. Occasionally we'd get a pair of newlyweds on the groom's dream vacation, but Cooke Pass did not seem to be too high on very many "Family Friendly Winter Vacation Destinations" lists. Add to that the facts that most people who lived in Cooke Pass and nearby Cooke City lived there only during summer and that Jacy and I were home schooled, and it did work out to be a rare event for my sister and me to hang around with other kids our age.

Listening to Jacy and these particular other kids talk nonstop for the past forty-five minutes about so much airy nothing though, had just about convinced me that it was really no big loss.

Movies. Fashion. The weather in California.

Who really cared?

"Are you going to ask the blessing on the food, Dakota?" my sister asked me. Then she turned her attention back to Amberlee and Cullen. "My brother's not real big on small talk."

While Amberlee and Cullen stared at me, I thanked God for the food and asked Him to bless it. Then I glared at my sister. She didn't have to apologize for me as if it were some kind of sin to not care about what colors are supposed to be "hot" next season.

"So what *does* your brother like to talk about?" Amberlee asked Jacy, looking at me the way a scientist might look at a piece of anomalous evidence.

"He's a mountain man," Cullen answered. "He likes to talk about hunting, fishing, bears, 4 x 4s, blizzards, and annoying know-it-all city people."

I laughed. That did pretty much sum it up.

"Hunting is barbaric," Amberlee said.

I didn't comment. She was entitled to her opinion.

"Meat is meat." My sister pointed the tip of her knife toward Amberlee's steaming steak dinner. "It's just a question of getting your own or buying the stuff from someone else who killed the animal."

Amberlee moved her fork to poke at her salad.

"My father says this is a great place for snowmobiling," Cullen put in after enjoying a couple bites of his steak. "You think our machines will do all right on these trails?"

Relieved that someone had finally chosen a subject worth talking about, I said, "Oh yeah. Your machines are the best they're making right now."

The Wheatleys had arrived in Cooke City in a shiny new SUV. After walking around it and making sure nobody was looking toward me, I'd gotten down on my side in the snow beside it to have a look underneath. Sure enough, it had everything. Skid plates. Heavy-duty axles. Big knobby lifted tires. After getting to my feet again and brushing the snow from my pants with my gloved hands, I'd walked back to the tarp-covered trailer they'd hauled up to get started on unloading their things.

I had to give the Wheatleys credit. Towing a trailer all the way through Yellowstone Park and up to Cooke City in the middle of winter was no small feat—not even for a shiny new SUV.

Since the Beartooth Highway was not plowed beyond the edge of Cooke City from the Park side during winter, Dad, Jacy, and I had driven snowmobiles over from Cooke Pass to meet the Wheatleys. They'd have to leave their outfit parked behind one of the gas stations in Cooke City during their stay with us, and we'd be getting around almost entirely by snowmobile. Jacy and I had ridden down on two of our smaller machines, and Dad had driven one of the bigger ones towing a sled to haul the Wheatleys' things back up to our place for them. It had been my job to strap all the Wheatleys' bags onto the sled—a duffle bag each for Cullen and his dad and an entire set of luggage for Amberlee, done in what was undoubtedly the most recent designer pattern available.

When I'd finished with the luggage and had made sure it was secure—since I'd be the one to have to retrieve it if it came loose and tumbled down the slope during the drive back—I'd gone back over to the Wheatleys' trailer to take a good look at their snowmobiles.

Again, nothing but the best. They'd do more than "all right" up here. They'd easily beat any of our machines both in speed and in maneuverability.

"I imagine you know all the trails up here?"

I looked across the table at Cullen and nodded.

"And you probably know the good places to go off trail?"

"We don't go off trail," Jacy and I told him in unison.

3

He laughed and winked. "Of course not."

"I hate snowmobiling," Amberlee said. "We only have two weeks a year with our dad, and this is where he takes us." She slid her platter of steak close to her again and began cutting at it with her sharp steak knife. "I mean, the man lives in Europe. We could be in Paris right now, or Madrid, or Rome. And here we are in some log restaurant on top of some boring mountain with nothing to do but freeze our toes off and shake our teeth out on snowmobiles."

I laughed. I couldn't help it. But Jacy, who was sitting beside me, elbowed me hard in the ribs.

"You only have two weeks a year with your dad?" she asked Amberlee.

"Yeah. Our parents are divorced, and we live in California with our mom."

"I'm sorry," Jacy said.

"Why? Everyone's parents are divorced."

I stopped laughing.

"Anyway," Jacy said, "we'll make sure you're dressed so that you'll be plenty warm out there."

"What about your mom?" Cullen asked. "I didn't see her at the house."

"She died when we were little," I told him, even though it was really none of his business.

"Oh," he said.

The four of us went quiet for a few minutes, and for the first time since we'd arrived at the café I became aware of the sound of wood popping in the big river rock fireplace behind me. I glanced over my shoulder at the fire, noticed it seemed to be struggling a little, and stood to add two small logs and another big one to it from the woodpile beside our table.

"Nothing like the warmth of a fire," Jacy said when I'd pulled my chair in beside hers again.

"Thanks, Dakota," the café's owner/cook/waiter/dishwasher/ maintenance man called to me from the kitchen.

I raised my hand. "No problem, Ken."

"The worst part of this whole vacation," Amberlee started in again, "is that it really isn't even a vacation because Dad's working."

I took a bite of baked potato. "What do you mean?"

"I mean he's working," she said louder, as if I were hard of hearing instead of confused. "This is what he does. He works for this hotshot resort-making company that goes around looking at little independent operations to see if they'd like to sell or merge or whatever. And then he turns them into bigger, fancier operations."

"Well, he's out of luck here," I assured her. "There's no way Dad would sell Back Trails."

"Maybe not," Cullen said. "But he must be thinking of at least merging. You know, selling a certain percentage of the ownership in Back Trails to my dad's company in exchange for my dad's company putting in the funds to turn your place into a winter haven for its very wealthy clientele."

"No way," I said, putting down my fork. "Your dad's just hoping, that's all."

"Your dad called my dad, Dakota. So he must be thinking—"

I shook my head. "No way."

"He didn't tell you guys?"

Jacy forced down a bite of her roll. "I'm sure we're missing something here," she said. "Dad wouldn't think about making changes to Back Trails without talking to Dakota and me first." She turned and looked at me. She didn't ask it, but I knew what she was thinking.

Would he?

I respected my father. He'd built a decent life and business for Jacy and me after mom had died, and he'd been turning himself inside out during the past few months since he'd become a Christian trying to learn how to really live for God.

But why would he have contacted Mr. Trevor Wheatley? And why would he have done so without talking to Jacy and me about it?

I couldn't see any sense in it.

Was he feeling worn out? Burned out? Stressed out?

Not that I could tell.

Was the business in trouble financially?

Not that I knew.

Was Dad worried about how he'd manage the business on his own during the next few years after first Jacy and then I left for college?

Not that I could imagine. He'd hired on help before when Jacy and I were still too little to help. He could easily do it again.

Besides, I wasn't even sure I wanted to go to college, and Dad knew that. I wanted to stay in Cooke Pass and do what I'd been doing pretty much my whole life—helping my father run his outfitting business and maybe take it over for him someday.

Keep Back Trails in the Craig family.

But Dad had his heart and mind set on Jacy and me going to college.

"Even if you do go just to come back and run Back Trails with me," he'd told me, "you'll be able to do it all that much better with a business degree under your belt."

That was probably true and I knew it, so I hadn't argued with Dad.

But now . . .

Could Cullen and Amberlee be right? Could Dad have called their father to discuss changes to Back Trails? Without talking to Jacy and me about it first?

No.

Jacy was right.

Cullen and Amberlee's father must have misunderstood our father. That was all.

Still, I could not finish my steak and had to sit there watching and waiting while Amberlee Wheatley managed to savor every last bite of hers.

CHAPTER 02

The sound of something scraping across the roof above my head woke me the next morning. A snow shovel. I knew without even having to open my eyes or turn my head toward my room's one window that a lot of new snow had come quietly during the night. We'd driven our snowmobiles home from Cooke City in the soft start of the storm when thousands of individual flakes fell huge and distinct in our headlight beams.

I got up. Dressed quickly. Put on my winter gear. And went outside to help my father.

And to talk to him.

He'd gone to his room already by the time Jacy, Cullen, Amberlee, and I had gotten back to the house after dinner, and other than a few brief words to me from the other side of his closed door about heading home a little earlier next time, he hadn't said anything.

"Morning," he said to me when I joined him on the roof with a snow shovel of my own. The air steamed in front of his words.

"Morning."

"Sleep good?"

I shrugged and scooped the shovel underneath a foot of new snow.

"Anyone else up inside?" he asked me.

"No, sir."

Another scoopful of snow. It was the wet heavy kind that felt like a pile of drenched sleeping bags on the end of a stick.

Dad shoveled. I shoveled. I wanted to ask him about what Cullen and Amberlee had told Jacy and me, but I wasn't sure how to go about it. I hoped he'd maybe volunteer the information—if, in fact, there was any truth to what they'd said. But he stayed quiet.

Quiet enough for long enough to chill me beyond the reach of the icy air.

"Dakota," he said finally, "I'm . . . uh . . . exploring the possibility of making some changes to Back Trails. Mr. Wheatley is in the business of—"

I lifted my hand from my shovel to interrupt him. "Cullen and Amberlee told us."

"They did?"

I nodded.

Neither of us was shoveling anymore.

"Well," he said, "it's just something I'm thinking about. Nothing definite yet. I wanted to wait to tell you and your sister until I'd seen his proposal, which I did last night. I knew how you'd feel about the idea, and I really didn't want to worry you about it if it was going to turn out that there was nothing to worry about anyway."

"So what's his proposal?" was all I could think to ask and all I knew I'd be able to say without sounding angry.

"I've asked him to talk to you and Jace about it after breakfast." And he left it at that.

The roof got cleared, and we went inside. Jacy met us with two cups of hot coffee, which we accepted and held tightly in our cold hands.

"I'm making French toast," she said to Dad. "Do you think the Wheatleys will like that, or should I . . . ?"

"French toast is fine," he said.

I sipped my coffee slowly while he told Jacy the same things he'd told me on the roof and then sat on a stool at the counter to pick at the breakfast she set in front of him.

"For now," he said to both of us, "I'm just looking at options, so relax. And please treat the Wheatleys like any other clients."

Jacy spoke first after several seconds of tense quiet. "Clients with some very sweet snowmobiles they're willing to share."

"They are nice machines," I had to admit.

"You're not kidding they are," Dad said.

We'd show the Wheatleys around Cooke Pass and the back country behind it. We'd take a look at their proposal. We'd ride some very expensive, very powerful toys. And while I relaxed and did all that, I'd pray that my father would decide not to think about doing business with Mr. Trevor Wheatley.

Pray about it.

"We should be praying about this," I said quietly, as much to myself as to my father and sister. "I mean, it's a big decision, and God certainly has a plan."

"You think He does?" Dad asked me. Genuinely. As if the possibility had never occurred to him.

"Why wouldn't He?" Jacy asked. "Our business is pretty much our whole life." Of the three of us, Jacy had been a Christian the longest. A little more than a year and a half. She always seemed to be the one pointing out what the Bible said or what Pastor Adams had told her once or what God might or might not want in a given situation.

Dad brought his empty coffee cup to the sink. "That's true. Our business is pretty much our whole life, so of course God would have a plan. So we'll all pray about this?" He turned back toward us. "About what we should do?"

What *we* should do.

"I'll pray," I promised him.

"Me too," said Jacy.

The three of us carried breakfast out to the dining room for the Wheatleys. While the three of them ate, Jacy and I looked with Dad at photos Mr. Wheatley had brought of some of his other resorts around the world. I couldn't imagine our place turning into anything even resembling them without major renovations . . . such as knocking it to the ground and starting over from scratch.

"Fancy places," Dad commented quietly when Mr. Wheatley had shown us all his photos and returned them to his briefcase. "The, uh, ambiance around here is decidedly more . . . uh . . ."

"Rugged?" Mr. Wheatley supplied.

"Yes," Dad said. "Rugged. And . . ."

Cullen leaned forward with his arms on the table. "Primitive?"

"Yeah." Dad nodded. "Well, no. Not primitive. But national parkish. You know."

Mr. Wheatley laughed out loud. "Hayden, one can secure accommodations at the national park down the road if one desires *national parkish*. This place would be for the more discerning traveler. The guest who appreciates and enjoys the finer things in life and doesn't mind paying for them."

"Hm," was all Dad would say.

But Jacy made up for his silence with a barrage of questions.

Would these discerning travelers still want to go snowmobiling and hunting and four-wheeling and backpacking?

Would we have to burn candles and hang crystals and hire someone to do mud wraps and pedicures?

Would we be expected to install a sound system in order to provide a constant background noise of soothing ocean sounds?

Would we, the humble and national parkish Craig family, even be allowed to live here?

By the time she finished, everyone at the table was laughing.

Mr. Wheatley got to his feet to announce that we'd discussed enough business for one morning. "Don't want to give all that new powder time to melt," he said, "now do we?"

"No, sir," I said.

I knew good and well that the previous night's snow wasn't going to go anywhere anytime soon, but the mention of it was as good an excuse as I needed to hurry out of the dining room to get into my winter gear and make myself comfortable on one of Mr. Wheatley's machines.

CHAPTER 03

"This is Wilderness Area," I called out across the snow to Cullen Wheatley. "You have to stay on the groomed trails."

He waved at me and then drove his snowmobile right off the trail and onto the meadow clearing where I'd just told him only two minutes earlier we were not allowed to ride.

As if nobody would see his ski and fancy pivoting tracks crisscrossing all over the forbidden snow.

It was people like him who ruined everything for law-abiding and boundary-respecting people like me. Some ranger would drive by and see that, put in a complaint to one of the guys with ties way up high on the government ladder somewhere, and the next thing we'd know there'd be a map coming out—a mandatory purchase—with all the designated trails . . . in ever decreasing numbers . . . marked in red, and a ten-thousand-dollar fine to be paid by anyone who went off them and got caught. Eventually they'd make the designated trails so difficult to get to and so far away from each other that it wouldn't be worth the bother anymore. Dad would be out of business. People would no longer be able to experience our nation's back country. The bears, who slept all winter anyway, would be free to roam. Environmentalists could come watch the one or two species of birds hearty enough to survive the area's winters—if, that is, they felt like hiking twenty miles through waist-deep snow to do it, which, of course, they wouldn't. And the forest rangers would become nothing more than revenue agents and snowmobile confiscators, penalizing the few people who'd go snowmobiling anyway.

I watched Cullen for a few minutes and then sped up the trail ahead of him. Maybe he'd take it as a challenge. Or maybe he'd be afraid he'd get lost if he lost sight of me. Or maybe he'd ignore me and stay in the meadows until a ranger happened by to issue him a warning, or better yet, a fine.

I found myself praying for option number three . . . but then remembered that vengeance belonged to Him. Not me.

I smiled though when I glanced back over my shoulder to see my sister pulling her machine to the edge of the meadow. She climbed off of it, stomped through the snow to stand right in the path of Cullen's machine, and then gave him a sizable chunk of her opinion while she pointed steadily back toward the trail. I couldn't hear what she was saying over my machine's engine noise, but I had no doubt that it had nothing to do with flora or fauna. By the time Amberlee came around the corner behind her, Jacy had restarted her snowmobile and was heading up the trail toward me.

When we got back home and the two of us were hanging the snowsuits to dry on hooks in the supply room, I asked her what she'd said to Cullen.

She waved away the question with a disgusted sigh. "Like it made any difference. I've never had a client ignore me like that. He was off trail all day."

"I know," I said.

"He's so . . . arrogant," she said.

"I know," I said again.

"And Amberlee doesn't do anything but complain."

"But hey, she is cute," I said, mostly to lighten Jacy's mood. "That's got to count for something, right?"

Jacy smiled and threw a pair of goggles at me. Hard. Then she asked me why I thought Dad had called Mr. Wheatley.

"Your guess is as good as mine, Jace."

She kept looking at the wall in front of her while she pulled one of the legs of Cullen's snowsuit down and straight.

"You could ask him," I suggested.

She hung Cullen's fancy ski cap next to his snowsuit. "So could you."

I set the gloves in pairs along the shelf above the coat hooks. "Maybe Mr. Wheatley will be just as disrespectful of the law during his ride with Dad as Cullen was, and we won't have to worry about it anymore because Dad'll send him packing."

Jacy shrugged. "I guess we can hope."

If either of us did hope, it ended up being for nothing. Dad and Mr. Wheatley returned from their snowmobile run laughing and joking and talking like two guys who'd known each other since high school.

It wasn't like my father to be quite so sociable, so I supposed he was pouring it on in order to impress Mr. Wheatley.

That wasn't like Dad either, and the sight of him doing it put a taste in my mouth like old milk.

"Did you kids have a good ride?" he asked me after struggling for several seconds to get out of his pullover ski coat.

I could barely manage a noncommittal shrug.

"It was fun, Mr. Craig," Amberlee said from the spot on the couch that she hadn't budged from since we'd gotten back. "But I'm only just now starting to feel warm again."

"Nobody could keep up with me," Cullen bragged. Lied.

I stepped right up next to Dad. "Only because he kept going off trail."

"Ah, you know," Dad said, "it can be tough to keep track of trails and of where it's Wilderness as opposed to National Forest."

"We told him the difference, Dad." I waited for Dad or Mr. Wheatley to comment, but neither man did.

Jacy excused herself from the conversation. It was time to get dinner started.

I followed her into the kitchen and shut the door between us and everyone else. "What is up with Dad? He made me memorize the whole stinking map last year so I'd know exactly where the boundaries between Wilderness and National Forest are. He knows I know it."

"I don't know." Jacy had done her fair share of map memorizing too. "But we've got to figure it out before he signs anything."

"We shouldn't worry." I crossed the room to the sink and filled a glass with water. "Dad always makes pretty good decisions, and we are all praying about this whole business thing."

Jacy came to stand beside me. "I know. But Dad just isn't acting like himself." She looked up at me. "You should talk to him, Dakota. Man to man."

"Yeah, right."

"I mean it."

Again, "Yeah, right."

But after the rest of the day with the Wheatleys discussing possible floor plans and staff requirements and gourmet food, I knew that I'd have to try. Mr. Wheatley had asked Dad what was involved with securing a license to sell alcohol in a business like ours, and Dad had said he'd check into it as if he'd been asked about the price of tomato paste at the general store.

We'd never served alcohol at Back Trails. Ever. Not even before we'd become Christians. I felt fairly certain that we shouldn't start doing so now.

How to point this out to Dad . . . something that seemed obvious enough to not need pointing out . . . and when? That's what I spent the whole evening trying to figure out. We ate dinner. We put away the snowmobiles for the night. We cleaned up the kitchen. We talked some more with the Wheatleys. And then Dad went upstairs to turn in for the night, telling me over his shoulder as he left that I was in charge of keeping the wood stove going until morning.

It wasn't the difficulty of the assignment that bothered me. It just required getting up every couple hours to throw in another couple of logs from the woodpile outside the back door. Simple. It was my job whenever Dad was away from the house during winter with clients. But I couldn't recall a time when he'd asked me to do it when he was home.

That's what bothered me.

It seemed to bother Jacy too. She looked up from the book she'd been showing Cullen, watched Dad for a couple seconds on the stairs, and then turned to me and mouthed *go.*

I got to Dad's door just in time to keep it from being closed in my face by holding out my hand. "Have you got a second?" I asked my father, who I couldn't see behind the door.

He stepped back to let me by his door and then closed it. Then he stood there waiting and looking almost tired enough to ask me if it couldn't wait until morning.

"You can't seriously be thinking about doing business with this guy," I said.

He sat on the edge of his bed and leaned forward over his knees to start unlacing his work boots. He said nothing.

"They ride off trail in Wilderness Area. They want you to serve alcohol. They want to . . ." I waved my hand, trying to think of the right word. "Dad, they want to totally redefine what Back Trails is."

He didn't look up from his laces. "They'd rename it."

"And that's okay with you?"

He yanked his boot off and tossed it in the general direction of the open closet door. "Maybe."

I sat beside him, wanting to grab hold of his arm when he reached down to start unlacing his other boot so that he'd stop what he was doing and look at me, but my hands stayed in my lap. "What's going on with you, Dad?"

For several long moments he worked at his laces. Struggled with them. They were wet and didn't want to slide free of the double knot he'd tied them into. But they came loose eventually.

"You know that the guy killed in last month's avalanche left behind a wife and three little kids?" Even when his second boot landed on the floor beside the other one, Dad didn't look at me.

"I didn't know that," I said. I did know about the avalanche. Everyone in the mountains on this side of the Park did. Four out-of-staters had been high marking up on Lulu Pass and had brought hundreds of tons of snow down on themselves. Three of the men had been buried but rescued. The fourth man's body had not yet been found and probably wouldn't be recovered until spring thaw.

High marking would be a thrill to be sure. Driving your snowmobile as fast as it would go up the steepest, most vertical slope you could find, pushing it and your strength to the limit to see how high up on the mountain you could get and still turn her around before she simply wouldn't go any further. But the problem with high marking was that almost all nearly vertical slopes had tons and tons of snow overhanging the side of the mountain. Tons of snow that could come crashing down if one of the machines or the noise unsettled it. Tons of snow that made high marking a risky venture.

A venture that my father never pursued and never allowed us or any Back Trails clients to pursue.

"I'm not always going to be around, Dakota," Dad said, "and I—"

"You don't take risks like that. You're always care—"

"And I'm just looking to get the business into a more stable situation so that you and your sister wouldn't lose it or have to move away from here if you didn't want to if something did happen to me."

18

"This is midlife crisis." I smiled, finally willing to nudge my father's arm. "I've read about this. And it's normal. But nothing's going to happen to you."

Dad responded by getting to his feet, walking across the room, and pulling open his door. "A *man* would understand these things. Good night, son."

"Dad—"

"Dakota," he said quietly, "I'm tired. Please respect me on this."

"All right." I stood up. He'd challenged my manhood and had dismissed me. What more could I say? Before passing by him on my way out to the hallway, though, I did stop and look right at him. "The idea is fine, Dad. I just don't think the Wheatleys are the solution. And there's no rush. It's not like it's them and their plan or nothing."

Dad stared at me—into me—for long enough that I would've bet my boots he had something more to tell me. But all he said when he finally did speak was, "See you in the morning."

CHAPTER 04

I did not see Dad the next morning. I woke up early and volunteered to drive the Wheatleys into Yellowstone Park for the day in order to show them some of the sights they hadn't had access to on their way in with their trailer. Mr. Wheatley declined, saying that if you'd seen one national park you'd pretty much seen them all, but Cullen and Amberlee seemed genuinely glad for the opportunity.

Jacy thought she might like to come with us, but decided to stay behind when Dad still hadn't come downstairs after the rest of us had finished eating breakfast. "I heard him up a couple times last night," she explained, "and I want to be sure he's okay."

I could have spared her the anxiety by letting her know that Dad was just stressing himself out because of the guy who'd died in the avalanche, but I didn't want to discuss it in front of the Wheatleys, and so I stayed silent. She'd figure it out. Or better yet, maybe Dad would get over it before Jacy learned anything about it.

Cullen, Amberlee, and I rode Back Trails snowmobiles down our unplowed driveway and the unplowed road that ended at the unplowed highway.

"Do you want to see Cooke Pass?" I asked them when they'd both pulled in alongside me before turning since it was to the left and Cooke City, Silvergate, and the northeast entrance to Yellowstone were all to the right.

"Is it worth seeing?"

I shrugged. "It's little. A few cabins is pretty much all."

Amberlee nodded. Cullen said, "Sure."

Their response surprised me given their father's attitude about seeing Yellowstone. It surprised me enough that I decided to give them one more day's chance to show me their decent side. If they couldn't manage it within the next several hours, though, they'd be forever labeled as idiots in my mind, and I wouldn't even feel guilty about it.

Even though I'd been a Christian for almost a year and a half, it was still hard sometimes to remember to try to think like one. Even—and maybe especially—toward people like the Wheatleys. Everything about them irritated me. Their attitudes. Their totally out-of-control egos. And now that I was aware of it, their whole reason for being at Back Trails in the first place. But God would want and expect me to think past all those things and to focus instead on the one thing that would actually matter a hundred years from now.

"So, Cullen," I asked him before pushing my machine's throttle, "do you believe in God?" I regretted how random that probably sounded to him and to his sister. Random and blunt, not to mention none of my business. But I had to start somewhere. "I mean, you know, do you guys go to church?"

"No. And no."

Plain enough.

Completely blank as to where to take the conversation next. I let it go and pulled my snowmobile out onto the unplowed highway and drove ahead of them around a couple curves, past a couple of empty summer houses, and then stopped. "Here's town."

Amberlee looked first to her right and then across the road to her left. Then she laughed. "This is it?"

I laughed too. "Yep."

"I couldn't imagine living here," Cullen said. Not insultingly. Just matter-of-factly. And that was fine. I couldn't imagine him living in Cooke Pass either.

We turned our machines around and drove into Cooke City. When we pulled in at the station where we'd be parking our snowmobiles and getting into the green Back Trails SUV that Dad always left parked in town during winter, Cullen started laughing and pointing. "Is that girl retarded or something?"

Megan Dassinger was shoveling snow outside the station her parents owned and operated. They'd moved to Cooke City only a few months earlier, and we'd invited them out to the house for dinner to get to know them and to welcome them. Dad liked knowing all the business owners in the area, and Jacy and I were excited to meet another teenager who'd actually be staying in town through the winter. Megan did move a bit awkwardly, and her smile was a bit crooked, which were undoubtedly the things about her that had captured Cullen Wheatley's attention. What he couldn't know without meeting her and would never guess because of his own arrogant ignorance was that Megan was smart, pretty, quick-witted, and loved God. She was rapidly becoming one of my best friends. My only friend that lived nearby.

"She has cerebral palsy," I explained to Cullen, "and she's a friend of mine. Have you got a problem with that?"

"No," he said. "Not at all." But he kept laughing.

"Is she your girlfriend?" Amberlee wanted to know.

I left her alone to wonder while I walked across the parking lot to say hello to Megan and to get our outfit started and the heater going.

Megan met me halfway. "Heading into Yellowstone for the day?"

"Yeah."

"I could make it a foursome," she said.

I leaned close to her to whisper, "I doubt you'd like the company."

She smiled. "Snobs?"

"You don't know the half of it."

"Oh, I bet I do."

I tugged her neon pink snow cap down over her eyes. "Okay. Maybe you do. But there's no need for you to subject yourself to it this time."

"I can't go anyway." She slid her hat up into place again and tucked her bangs back underneath it. "I've got to shovel the lot."

We went inside the station together where I nodded across the counter at Mr. Dassinger. "My dad could rig something up for you . . . put a scoop on one of your four-wheelers. You could fire it up and plow the lot. It'd be a lot faster."

Megan yanked my hat down over my eyes and then pushed it back again. "I like to shovel. It's good exercise."

Who could argue with that? I raised my hand to Megan and her father, walked back outside onto the half-cleared lot, said hello to a couple of tourists with a trailer full of snowmobiles, taking the time to tell them where the best trails were, and then joined Cullen and Amberlee in our SUV where I climbed in behind the wheel.

We drove in silence for a while before I told them that the only road open during winter was the one they'd come in on. So to see some of the other sights, like Old Faithful, we'd be borrowing three snowmobiles from an outfitter friend of Dad's once we got to Mammoth. "Did you guys see any wildlife on your way over?"

Cullen shrugged. "Elk."

"Mountain sheep?"

"No."

"We'll try to creep up behind some of them without spooking them."

"Thrills," Amberlee said.

It turned out to be the worst day I could ever remember having in Yellowstone Park. Even worse than the time I'd spent the whole drive home throwing up after falling out of the back of Dad's pickup and smacking my head on the pavement. Amberlee was whiny. Cullen was about as interesting to talk to as a potato, and almost everything he said was insulting.

What's so great about the bison herds anyway that they need to preserve all this land for them? They're ugly.

The Alps are much more majestic than these mountains.

Whatever.

When we pulled into Dad's friend's parking area, I thought I might be more appreciative of the snowmobile ride, if only for the simple fact of not having to endure any more conversation.

Ted Severson met us outside his shop, wearing his usual sheepskin vest, blue jeans, cowboy boots, and moldy, dirty hat. He walked as if he'd just climbed down off a horse even though he probably hadn't been on one since the fall elk season. "Howdy, boys," he said. Then he tipped his hat for Amberlee's benefit.

I cringed. These two big-city teenagers were about to experience meeting a true Montana cowboy who had nothing pressing to do but stand around and shoot the breeze.

"Got 'em filled up for you. They're ready to roll."

Cullen squinted down at the three machines parked in front of us. "Are you sure these will ever be ready to roll?"

The machines were decent, adequate, but not nearly as fancy as the ones Cullen was accustomed to.

Mr. Severson grinned. "Looks like you've got your day cut out for you, Dakota."

I nodded.

With a wave of his hand and another tip of his hat aimed mostly at me, Mr. Severson turned and went back inside his shop.

"You know," I said to Cullen, "he's doing us a favor letting us use these machines. You could have been grateful."

Cullen shrugged, climbed onto his machine, took a couple seconds to familiarize himself with it, and started her up. He revved on the gas before the machine had warmed up, causing it to pour out clouds of blue smelly exhaust. "Are you sure these are going to get us back here?" he asked, waving his hand in front of his face, gagging and laughing.

"It'd certainly have a chance if you took care of it like you would your own machine." After making Cullen wait through more than enough time for the machines to warm up, I led the way to Old Faithful, the most famous geyser in the world. The subject of thousands of pictures and videos and entire documentaries. Famous for her faithfulness at erupting approximately every seventy minutes or so, Old Faithful spews boiling hot water a hundred and thirty feet into the air in a towering, steaming, hissing fountain. All of which failed to impress Cullen even though I thought the geyser looked even more awesome in the winter because of all the extra steam in the icy cold air.

Amberlee seemed to enjoy it, though she didn't say so.

When we finished there, I agreed to let Cullen lead the way back since there was really no way he could get lost on the clearly marked trail.

Big mistake.

Not only did Cullen not yield to the occasional oncoming traffic of other snowmobilers and big snow cats hauling tourists, but when there was no oncoming traffic, he sped, completely ignoring the Park's posted fifty-five miles-per-hour speed limit signs. I had warned him before we'd started out that the rangers in Yellowstone used radar guns to catch snowmobilers speeding, but he'd apparently concluded that he didn't need to clutter his mind with such concerns.

I stayed right behind him, but he never let me catch up to him. Probably because he knew I'd insist on taking the lead back over. I was aware that Amberlee wasn't keeping up with me, but

I didn't slow down to wait for her. She'd catch up eventually. I felt like my first responsibility was to try to rein in Cullen.

But barring going even faster than he was to pull out ahead of him and stop short in front of him, which I wasn't about to attempt on the narrow trail, there was no way for me to stop him.

The angry looks he got from oncoming drivers didn't stop him either.

It took a Park ranger to do that.

A Park ranger who appeared seemingly out of nowhere from behind the snow mounds alongside the trail. A Park ranger undoubtedly equipped with radar. A ranger who knew exactly how fast we'd been traveling.

If I had seen him, I would have slowed down to let Cullen face the consequences of his actions alone. But I didn't see him until he'd already seen me.

We'd get fined for sure. Speeding in the Park.

"Dad's going to kill me," I whispered as I pulled up alongside Cullen to wait for the ranger.

Cullen squinted at me. "What?"

"I wasn't talking to you," I snapped at him.

The ranger, who of course knew Dad, asked Cullen and me several questions while he filled in blanks in his ticket pad before handing us each our own slip. He told us that he was going easier on us than he might otherwise have because he'd never known Dad or Jacy or me to speed in the Park before, because Cullen, a client, had been ahead of me and I might have felt obligated to keep up with him, and because we'd caught him in a good mood.

I glanced quickly at the slip of paper in my gloved hand before folding it clumsily in half and shoving it deep into my coat pocket. Easy on us or not, the fine was significant. I wondered if the ranger had issued Cullen the same fine. Maybe he'd issued him a bigger one.

Cullen laughed when he glanced at his slip of paper. "You going to come to California to get this from me if I don't pay it?"

I was too stunned to flash Cullen the look of contempt he deserved.

The ranger, however, was not stunned at all. "Let me see that." He snatched the slip of paper right back out of Cullen's hand. He crossed something out and marked something else in its place. "This is the maximum I'm allowed to fine you," he said, "and I do suggest you pay it."

Now I had no doubt that Cullen's fine was bigger than mine.

Not that that would matter to my father.

"You lead the way the rest of the way out," the ranger said to me.

"Yes, sir."

"And say hello to your father for me."

"Yes, sir. You bet."

The ranger left, and since we had to wait for Amberlee anyway, I decided to tell Cullen to bring more brains and less cockiness along the next time I took him somewhere. He was a client, yes, and under normal circumstances I didn't criticize clients, but this was not a normal circumstance, and I had the ticket in my pocket to prove it. If Cullen whined to his father and his father whined to my father, Dad would side with me. I was sure of it.

Speeding in the Park was against the law.

When Amberlee finally caught up to us, I pulled my machine into the lead on the trail and headed back toward Mr. Severson's place.

In spite of the slip of paper in my pocket, I did enjoy the ride. It had been a while since I'd driven in Yellowstone Park just to sightsee. We drove through it several times a year to get out of the mountains for supplies since it was sometimes the only route available to us, but that wasn't the same as driving to sightsee. And seeing the Park from a snowmobile offered its own right-there-in-the-thick-of-things perspective. A person tended to spot a lot more wildlife in the winter than in the summer because fewer trails and roads were open and there were fewer tourists. Plus the high country grew a lot more brutal and moody during winter, forcing much of the wildlife down closer to the valleys where people on snowmobiles could see them . . . walking, sleeping, playing, eating their prey.

After everything we'd seen in the Park, the only thing that seemed to inspire any excitement or appreciation from Cullen Wheatley was a pack of coyotes devouring an elk carcass alongside the trail. He actually stopped to snap a picture of the gruesome scene.

Back at the shop, we parked the machines. I thanked Mr. Severson for letting us borrow them and then paid him for the gas we'd used. He and Dad had an agreement about sharing machines, both snowmobiles and ATVs, and frequently brought clients back and forth.

It started to snow shortly after I pulled out in Dad's SUV with the heater set to max. The snow came softly at first in big flakes that too soon turned smaller and meaner. I spent the whole afternoon focusing on the glimpses I could catch of the narrow gray strip of road ahead through sheets and sheets of blowing swirling snow. White. Dense. Heavy. It clouded out all the scenery and whitened my knuckles on the steering wheel.

Amberlee, who was sitting in the front passenger seat only because I'd insisted to Cullen that he let his sister have it for the ride home since he'd taken it on the way in, asked me if we maybe should pull over and wait it out.

"It could snow for days," I told her. "If it ends up that we do have to stop, it'll be better to be closer to home so Dad can find us quicker."

"Are you sure?" She sounded a little scared.

"We're going to make it home fine," I tried to assure her. "It's just going to take a little longer is all."

She must not have been convinced, because she asked me again if I was *sure* I was sure we shouldn't stop.

"Quit being such a baby," her brother demanded from the back seat. "Dakota drives in this kind of stuff all the time. Right, Dakota?"

"I drive in it enough that I'll know when I need to stop." I turned my attention from what little I could see of the road ahead and looked quickly at Amberlee. "Okay? We'll be okay."

Slowly, she nodded.

And she didn't ask me anymore whether I thought we should stop.

It snowed all afternoon. All the way home. If it wasn't for the fact that the plows left mounds on both sides of the road, I might have wrecked during a couple stretches where the snow hid even the occasional glimpse of the road. But I was determined to keep driving. To keep from having to pull over and wait out the sudden blizzard.

Cullen and Amberlee were Back Trails clients, and it was my job to get them safely back.

So that's what I did.

Getting out of the warm SUV and back onto snowmobiles at Cooke City was miserable. The machines were cold. The snow was cold. And so was the dark of night. I felt nothing but relief when we stopped our snowmobiles in front of our house.

But Cullen managed to make being home even more miserable than being in the park during a blizzard had been by teasing me all through dinner about my "wobbly little girlfriend" at the gas station and laughing about my having to settle for her because she was the only girl my age within a hundred miles.

Amberlee told him to shut up a couple times, but his father did nothing.

I wanted to punch him. More than anything else, I wanted to punch Cullen Wheatley.

So much anger tightened my muscles that I couldn't even think of another response. I didn't deny that Megan was my girl-friend, even though she wasn't. I didn't defend her, or tell Cullen to quit insulting her, even though that's probably what I should have done. I couldn't even think clearly beyond the fact of how satisfying it would feel to slam my fist into his proud annoying little mouth.

Somehow I kept my right hand around my fork and my left hand in my lap, knowing with a certainty that God would not be pleased by my punching Cullen even if that's what he deserved.

At one point after a particularly rude remark by Cullen, I glanced across the table to find my father staring at me with his forkful of food held halfway between his plate and his mouth.

I knew what he was doing because he did this kind of thing all the time.

He was waiting for me to do what a man would do. Giving me a split second of opportunity to do it before he stepped in to do it for me.

All I could think that most men would do in this situation was pound the loser . . . and yet I knew that was not the response that my father was waiting for from me.

The only trouble was, I couldn't come up with any other re-sponse.

Not one.

So my father lowered his fork to his plate again and turned his attention squarely to Cullen. "Son," he said stiffly but quietly, "Megan Dassinger is a human being just like you. She's just as valuable as you. She was created by the same God Who created you. You will not disrespect her at this table or in this house."

And that was that.

Cullen shut up and finished his peas.

Dad went back to his food.

So did Jacy, Amberlee, and Mr. Wheatley.

And so did I.

But I knew that I had failed. I'd had the opportunity to be a man. My father had given me the opportunity to be a man. And I'd blown it. Maybe on a different day, a day not spent trying not to be rude, the correct response to Cullen's teasing would have come easily to me. But just as likely maybe not. The only thing that mattered, and the only thing that was certain, was that I had not been able to come up with it when it counted.

I helped Jacy clear the table and do the dishes after dinner and then stayed in the kitchen by myself trying to come up with a workable strategy for telling Dad about my speeding ticket. After a while I had to wonder who I thought I was kidding. Strategy. What strategy? I could be in a full body cast when I presented the ticket to my father, and it wouldn't make a bit of difference. He'd be silent while he considered his options for punishing me, and then he'd punish me, and that would be that.

I decided that the best thing to do was find my father, hand over the ticket, wait silently for his verdict, and then take it like a man with a simple *yes sir.*

After all, I had been speeding in the Park.

With my right hand in my pocket around the folded slip of paper, I walked through the house until I finally found Dad in the supply room.

"Hey," he said when he heard me come in. He didn't turn to look at me.

I shut the door. "Hey."

He was standing in front of the shelves where we kept our backpacking equipment, tightening the end of one of our tent sacks. I was about to ask him what he was doing since we were still several months out from any kind of decent camping weather—at least with that particular tent—when he said, "This is the first tent I ever brought up here."

"Yeah, it's old," I said. "I think it leaks in a couple places. And some of the stake straps are bro—"

"Your mother and I used to camp in this tent," he said, "when we first got married and would come up here for vacation." He slowly lifted his hand from the shiny material and turned to face me. "We used it when you and Jace were little too. Do you remember?"

I didn't remember. So I shook my head even though I didn't want to. I hated these moments of having to admit to my father that I didn't remember as much about my mother as he clearly wanted me to remember.

"Yeah." He said what he always said. "You were too little."

"Dad," I said, knowing what I had to do even though the fact that he was thinking about Mom would only make things harder on both of us, "I have something to tell you."

"Okay." He grabbed two of our foldup camp stools, shook them open, waited for me to sit on the one he handed me, and then sat down right in front of me. Within inches of me. "What?"

Keeping my mouth shut, I slid the still folded-up ticket from my pocket and held it out to him.

He took it. Unfolded it. Looked at it. Twice. Then looked at me. "How did this happen?"

I told him.

After only a moment, he refolded the ticket and slid it into his shirt pocket. "You keep the lead from now on, Dakota. Don't follow a person into doing something wrong."

"Yes, sir."

"I need to be able to trust you on this before I can let you start leading hikes this summer."

"Yes, sir."

"I need to be able to trust you on this, period," he said.

"Yes, sir." I stood up, folded the camp stool, and leaned it against the wall. "I'm sorry, Dad."

"Oh," he said, "not as sorry as you will be when the deck needs to be stained again this summer or when next winter's wood needs to be hauled, chopped, and stacked or when—"

I held up my hand to stop him. I got the point. "Yes, sir."

"Anything I ask you to do," he said, "we'll keep track of at minimum wage per hour until you've paid this off. It'll save me hiring guys on. This is a lot of money."

"I know."

"No complaining," he said. "And no putting things off."

I nodded.

Dad stood up, pushed his stool back, stepped toward me, and hugged me. "You've got to be smart out there, Dakota," he said as he dropped his arms and stepped back from me again. "That's what I'm trying to do with Back Trails and the Wheatleys."

The last thing I wanted to do at that particular moment was disagree with my father out loud, so I nodded as if I understood even though I didn't, said goodnight to him, and went upstairs to turn in for the night.

My alarm buzzed before dawn the next morning, and I shut it off quickly so it wouldn't wake anyone else. Quietly I got up, dressed, and went downstairs for a quick bowl of hot cereal before leaving.

I'd made up my mind that I needed a day to myself. And I'd made up my mind that I'd spend it cross-country skiing on some of the trails behind Cooke City. Up Republic Pass. I'd leave a note for Dad. I'd complete my school lessons that afternoon. He'd understand. And hopefully I'd be able to return home with some kind of proper perspective about the Wheatleys and Dad and this whole mess with the business.

Dad knew how I felt about Back Trails. He knew that I'd like to spend the rest of my life up here doing what he'd been doing—with him and then after him. He knew, and yet he was considering selling it—merging, combining, modifying, whatever—and making it into something that I'd rather beg on the street than be part of.

I couldn't eat my oatmeal, so I dumped it in the garbage and grabbed a handful of granola bars to bring along with me in case I got hungry or needed an energy boost later in the day.

The snowplow had been by already by the time I got to Cooke City even though it was still dark. I drove my snowmobile slowly along the mounds at the side of the trails, my headlights reflecting off thousands of dancing snowflakes. Peaceful. Not at all like the blizzard I'd driven through the day before. By the time I parked at the bottom of one of the trailheads and unstrapped my skis and poles from the sled, I was hungry.

I ate all the granola bars, got into my ski gear, strapped my insulated water bottle around my waist, and hit the trail.

The sun rose above the top of the mountain behind me as I made my way into the thick forest and started switchbacking up the trail. I pushed my pace to get my blood flowing and to work up a sweat because the temperature and falling snow were less than accommodating.

It didn't take long to warm up on the steep trail I'd chosen, and soon I'd weaved my way out of the trees and onto the meadows that lay still and serene in the gray light of snowy dawn.

By late morning, it quit snowing. I found some frozen creeks to jump over, some semisteep hills to ski down, and some challenging drifts to conquer. I pushed my way up past treeline and looked out across the vast expanse of frigid winter air between the spot where I stood and a spot about even with me on the side of the mountain across the valley. While I stood there catching my breath, the sun melted away the last of the moisture in the air around me, and I stood in perfect warm, bright, white light. The meadows below me sparkled at the sun's touch, and the whole valley seemed to awaken. The trees looked green instead of gray. I saw a big bull elk standing at the edge of a cluster of trees. He seemed to be trying, as I was, to absorb every aspect of these silent perfect moments.

I kept motionless so that he wouldn't see me and bolt. For nearly half an hour, the two of us stood there alone in the vast valley, watching. But then something caught his attention and he made his way back into the cover of the trees, and I headed further up the trail. I was getting cold again. The insides of my nose had begun to freeze together, and my ears burned even through my good-to-forty-below hat.

Standing still too long when the temperature couldn't have been above ten degrees.

But it had been worth it. Every second.

It occurred to me when I nearly lost my balance on a precariously slick section of switchbacks that skiing alone up here probably wasn't the wisest thing to do, and that Dad, even if he understood my need to escape the Wheatleys for a day, might not appreciate my reasoning—or apparent lack of it—when it came to choosing my means of escaping them. Especially after his comments the night before about being "smart out there" and about his needing to be able to trust me. If I fell up here and injured myself, nobody would know where I was or come looking for me. And by the time they did, I'd be frozen solid in a heap somewhere.

Rest in peace.

No wonder Dad hadn't felt compelled to consult with me about the business before inviting Mr. Wheatley to Cooke.

"Please help me get down safely," I prayed aloud, "and to not blow up at Dad when he chews me out for being stupid."

Amen.

As soon as I finished praying, I turned around on the switchbacks and started making my way down the mountain.

By noon I'd reached only the halfway point because it had warmed up and the sun had melted the top layer of snow into a glassy icelike surface that challenged me even though I was a decent enough skier. I enjoyed the long stretches of downhill through the trees on old logging roads, because they were wide enough to not pose any risk of slamming into anything. But much of the trail I'd chosen was just a ski trail switchbacking down through the trees, wide enough for only a person and sometimes not even that. I had to watch for branches at my eye level and boulders hidden underneath the snow. All while laboring to contain my speed to a level within the boundaries of my skill.

I'd been on the mountain for six hours and had not seen another human being.

The temperature finally warmed enough that I most likely wouldn't freeze to death if I fell and hurt myself, so I relaxed and again began savoring the challenge of conquering the trail and thereby the mountain. I quit trying to hold my skis back, ducked under low branches, and jumped lumps in the snow that might be boulders or stumps. I sped around the turns in the switchbacks, throwing powder into the trees, and once or twice even yelled out in triumph as I soared through the air.

Until I came around a sharp corner and plowed right into some guy coming up. The two of us tangled into a mess of skis and poles and crashed in a pile together at the base of a dead tree. I scrambled up and off of him as quickly as I could, wiped blood off my lip with my sleeve, and said, "Man, I'm so sorry. I didn't see you coming. Are you all right?"

The guy, who'd somehow ended up on his face in the snow even though he'd started our fall by being knocked off his feet backwards, rolled slowly onto his back and squinted as he held his hand out toward me.

Dad.

"Help me up," he said.

I did.

"I don't think you were in complete control," he said.

"No, sir."

"You should always be in complete control."

"Yes, sir."

"I'm glad it was me you slammed into and not someone waiting for a lawsuit opportunity."

"Me too," I said. "I mean, I'm not glad I ran into you, but—"

Dad laughed. "I know what you mean." He raised his gloved hand to my upper lip. "Looks like you're going to get a fat lip," he said. "Did a pole get you?"

"I couldn't even tell you." I raised my gloved hand to the outside corner of his left eye. "Looks like you're going to get a black eye."

"So we're even."

We set about to gather our poles and step back into our skis and then started heading down the trail together, Dad ahead of me, keeping the pace much slower than mine had been before I'd run into him.

"How'd you find me?"

"I putted around until I found your snowmobile and then took a guess at which trail you'd choose in your current frame of mind."

"Thanks," I said.

"Yeah."

We went the rest of the way down the mountain without any more conversation. I loaded my skis and poles back onto my sled, and Dad strapped his skis and poles to his, and then we drove our snowmobiles—me behind him—home.

There was never more than a few feet of snowy road separating me and Dad, but I was beginning to feel as if something huger than all the mountains was shoving its way between us and threatening to push us apart.

He hadn't even raised his voice when I'd crashed into him on that corner.

One would think that was a good thing, or at least a lucky break. But I knew it wasn't.

He should have yelled at me. Grounded me from skiing for the rest of the winter. Not only because I'd let myself go fast enough to be out of control on the mountain, but because I'd gone up there alone in the first place.

Jacy was right.

Dad was not acting like himself.

He hadn't even looked like himself when he'd stood in front of me on the mountain. He'd looked more scared than angry. Even his color hadn't looked right.

I knew it had something to do with the Wheatleys. And Back Trails. And that guy with kids who'd died in the avalanche. But I couldn't put it together. I couldn't see the connection.

And the worst part of all of it was that Dad almost certainly held the common thread tightly in his grasp but didn't trust me enough, didn't think I was man enough, to loosen his hold on it and show it to me.

Mr. Wheatley sat alone at the dining room table when I came downstairs the next morning. Early. He'd made himself a pot of coffee and was studying a Forest Service map of the area that he'd folded open in front of him.

"Do you suppose we could convince them to plow the road all the way in to Cooke Pass for us?" he asked me when he looked up and saw me.

"Doubt it," I said, even though I didn't have a clue whether or not such a thing could be arranged.

He frowned. "Some clients wouldn't want to ride in on a snowmobile."

"Well," I said, "there're plenty of hotels in Cooke City."

Mr. Wheatley raised his cup to his lips and said nothing.

I walked quickly to the kitchen to pour myself a cup of coffee and then returned to the dining room. I showed Mr. Wheatley on the map where some of my favorite snowmobile, backpacking, and ATV trails were and then asked him if Dad had mentioned that the Forest Service would eventually like to turn this whole area into a wilderness area where nobody could live and that was accessible only on foot.

He laughed. "No. He didn't mention that. Probably because it'll never happen." He sipped his coffee and stared at me while I shrugged. "They don't even want horses?"

"No," I told him. "It's already a lot more complicated than it used to be to bring horses in. You have to have the hay you'll be feeding them inspected because it might contain weeds that could eventually contaminate the area."

Mr. Wheatley's turn to shrug. "I guess that makes sense."

"Somehow the wilderness has survived just fine for more than a hundred years with horses and mules being led around hauling all the iron mining machinery up to the old mines. Nobody cared about the hay they ate then."

"They didn't know any better," Mr. Wheatley suggested, "and weren't as environmentally conscious as we are today."

"Most people around here would say *environmentally paranoid*," I said. "I mean, they've got rules about the kinds of engines you can have in your ATVs and dirt bikes. They can close any of the back roads at any time without any logical explanation except that they felt like it. They can restrict where you camp and whether or not you can have a campfire because it's too dry even though you can hardly walk along the trails or through the meadow grass without getting wet up to your knees. And you know some poor guy in a wheelchair can't go on some of the trails and have access to the National Wilderness Areas that his tax dollars pay for, not because the trail would be too difficult for him, but because his chair is a wheeled vehicle that might flatten some blades of grass."

"I've got to agree that's a bit silly," Mr. Wheatley said. "But then I suppose if you don't like your nation's laws, you could move somewhere else. China, maybe. Cuba."

Did this man have a brain the size of a walnut? I loved my country. The liberty to talk about laws and to pursue getting them changed if need be was one of the reasons. I decided to change the subject. "You heard about the fires in Yellowstone in 1988?"

Mr. Wheatley thought for a moment but then shook his head.

"They were started by lightning, so the guys in charge decided to let them burn since that's what would happen in nature. Only problem is that the Park has boundaries that didn't used to exist in nature. And once the fire crossed those boundaries, it threatened peoples' homes and whole towns. Cooke City was one of those towns. So what does the Forest Service do? The fire was about fifteen miles away from Cooke City at Storm Creek," I showed him on the map, "so they decide to set a backfire. Guess where they put it?"

Mr. Wheatley set his cup down on the map. "A couple miles up from Storm Creek?"

"No," I told him. "About four miles from here behind Colter Camp Ground. With Cooke City between it and the original fire. I mean, that's like starting a backfire in your living room if you have a kitchen fire. Plus they set fire to the old ghost town on Miller Creek—even though that's supposed to be against some kind of antiquities preservation law—to be sure it wouldn't create a hot spot. Then the backfire goes out of control and the Forest Service ordered all the residents of Cooke to evacuate, saying they'd fight the fire. About eighty percent of the people stayed and fought the fire themselves and kept the town itself from burning. But that's why there's all this burn area right around here."

"The residents didn't quite trust the Forest Service to contain the fire?"

I leaned forward and set my cup down on the map. "Let's just say that some of them figure the backfire was the Forest Service's way of moving itself one step closer to turning this whole area to wilderness."

"That's ridiculous," Mr. Wheatley said.

I shrugged. "I'm just telling you what some people think. And what you might want to think about before investing a whole lot of money in this area."

"So that's what this is all about." Mr. Wheatley moved his coffee cup aside, gestured for me to do the same with mine, and then quickly and competently refolded the map. "Your father did tell me that you aren't particularly excited about my proposal."

"Sir—"

"That's all right," he said. "No need to apologize. I like a boy who looks out for his father's interests. And for his own interests, since Back Trails might well have been yours someday."

Apologizing had been the furthest thing from my intention when I'd opened my mouth, but being interrupted had given me a couple seconds to reconsider telling Mr. Trevor Wheatley exactly how unexcited I truly was about his proposals and everything else about his visit.

I owed it to Dad to be respectful to this man even if neither he nor Dad were being particularly respectful of me. "I just don't think that what you have in mind for Back Trails is what we'd ever planned for it. We've always kind of geared our services toward people who want to get out in nature, not stay inside and be pampered in a house out in nature."

"Things grow." Mr. Wheatley clasped my shoulder as if he were my long-lost uncle or something. "Things change. And what it all comes down to this time, Dakota my boy, is how excited I can get *your father* about my proposal."

He didn't add *regardless of how you feel about it,* but he might as well have because bottom line, it was the truth.

Dakota my boy.

I stood and picked up both our cups. Before heading to the kitchen with them, I smiled down at Mr. Wheatley. It was the only way I knew to keep my face at least looking respectful because I sure wasn't having any success maintaining that brand of attitude. "Church this morning," I told him. "You guys want to come along?"

He answered right away. "No."

Good enough was my first thought. But still I said, "It's kind of a community chapel, mainly geared toward tourists, so you'll probably feel comfortable there no matter what denomination you are."

"I'm no denomination," he said, "of no religion."

I nodded. "So was I until a year and a half ago."

"How lovely for you." He pushed his chair back from the table, grunted as he got to his feet, and left the room without pushing his chair back in.

Well . . . I'd tried, right?

Our normal routine for Sunday mornings, whether we had clients at the house or not, was to fend for ourselves for breakfast. We prepared no official meal and always made sure our clients understood they could go to the kitchen and scrounge around for whatever suited them. Toast. Cereal. Eggs and bacon. Coffee. Milk. Juice. More often than not, when we did have clients at the house, they'd come to church with us if for nothing else than to experience the tourist-aimed service. During summer this worked well since we could all pile into one or two SUVs for the drive to Cooke City. Winter posed somewhat more of a challenge in that we had to get ourselves there on snowmobiles.

I had my tie just about tied when I tapped Dad's door with my elbow. "It's almost time to leave for church," I said loudly enough that I knew he'd hear me through the closed door. "Are you up?"

"Yeah, I'm up," came his hoarse reply from the other side of the door. Then there was a long silence. Long enough that I concluded he was getting ready and would pull open his door any moment and join me in the hallway, tying his tie. But he didn't. Instead he said, "Take your sister and go ahead without me this week, Dakota."

"Are you okay, Dad?" He'd been sick with the flu a couple weeks earlier and had spent most of Sunday and all of Monday in his room behind his closed door.

Again there was a pause. Not as long this time before he said, "I just want to sleep in today. Okay?"

44

The desire to sleep in, especially on a Sunday, was about as normal for my father as eating cucumber and cream cheese sandwiches. It never happened.

"Stay in and have lunch with the Dassingers if you want," he added. "Trevor and I are going to be running numbers all morning. Boring stuff and nothing I need your help with. You might as well stay busy in town."

So that was it.

My father intended to skip church to *run numbers* with Mr. Wheatley.

And here I'd been worried about his having the flu again. As if a person would get the flu twice in a month.

I walked away from his closed door.

CHAPTER 07

Cullen Wheatley met me at the bottom of the stairs after I'd pounded on Jacy's door and told her to hurry up.

"My dad says you're heading to church?"

"Yeah." I wasn't in the mood for any condescending guff from Cullen, and I put an expression on my face that would more than adequately communicate that message. "So?"

"Can I go with you? We could go riding afterwards?"

I felt badly about my bad attitude, but not enough to think it warranted an apology since Cullen Wheatley was sure to provoke it again before the day was out. "Sure," I said, "you can come. And we can go riding all afternoon if we want, because our dads are going to be talking business."

He smiled. "Great. I want to go see where that avalanche happened—the one that everyone's been talking about."

I hadn't been up on that part of the mountain since the avalanche, and even though it might be somewhat morbid, I couldn't deny being curious to see it myself. I'd been to other avalanche sites, of course, and had even helped with search and rescue at a couple of them. I knew that enough new snow had fallen between this most recent avalanche and now, that most of the interesting and eerie aftermath would be covered and smoothed over. They'd already regroomed the trails, and tourists who had no idea about what had happened had already driven their snowmobiles back and forth over almost the exact place where two of the three survivors had been dug out. That's the way both nature and business worked.

Cullen, Jacy, and I drove to church on three separate snowmobiles. Jacy didn't want to go riding with us afterwards. She wanted to be home near Dad. She rode one of Back Trails' snowmobiles, Cullen rode his own, and I rode Mr. Wheatley's.

Church was poorly attended that morning, by regulars or tourists, probably because of all the recent new snow. It would have dissuaded all but the most hearty from venturing to the Park for another couple of days.

In spite of the low attendance, or maybe on account of it, the new young pastor, who was really more of a forest-ranger-loner-type with lots of Bible knowledge, preached a strong message out of one of the books of Kings about restitution. If you borrow something and damage or lose it, you're responsible to replace it. Saying "I'm sorry" isn't good enough. If you sin against someone, it's your responsibility to go to them and attempt to make it right. If you owe money, pay it. Things like that. Not particularly encouraging or discouraging. Just common sense instruction on the right way to live. Nothing that pertained to me personally since, apart from the speeding ticket I'd just gotten, I didn't owe any money and in general Dad and Jacy and I didn't borrow things.

Of course I would be riding Mr. Wheatley's snowmobile all afternoon. But I felt fairly confident that I could keep from damaging it by driving responsibly. I'd have to keep from damaging it, I knew, because I'd have to sell everything I actually owned and still borrow several thousand dollars more from Dad to pay for it if I did wreck it.

As I sat in church, I began to wish I'd driven one of our machines instead, but as soon as I stepped outside at the end of the service I was glad I'd borrowed one of the Wheatleys'. Their machines were a lot newer than ours. A lot more powerful and equipped with a lot more goodies including a pivoting track, built-in hand and feet warmers, three cylinder heads instead of two, and seats that were actually comfortable. Their machines could go from standing still to sixty quickly enough to snap your head back!

"Nice snowmobiles," Pastor Blake said. He seemed to have followed me outside deliberately. He stood beside me, tucking the cuff of his glove up inside his coat sleeve. "Going riding?"

"Yeah."

"I didn't see your dad this morning," he said.

"That's because he's home," I said.

"He's not sick again, is he?"

"No, sir."

"Well," the pastor said, concerned—and with good reason considering that Dad had not missed a single Sunday service since he'd become a Christian other than when he'd had the flu, not even during hunting season—"that's good anyway."

I supposed that was one way to look at it.

"I'll give your dad a call later," Pastor Blake said as he turned and hurried away from us.

"Thanks," I called after him, meaning it.

I led the way out of town. Before passing us when Cullen and I turned onto Lulu Pass, Jacy pulled alongside me to unstrap the foldup shovel from the side of her machine and toss it to me.

"Just in case you get stuck or something," she said.

I hadn't noticed that the Wheatleys didn't carry any emergency gear on their machines. No shovels, first-aid kit, waterproof matches. Things we always carried with us.

I strapped the shovel to the small rack behind my seat.

"Keep your eyes open," she said.

I nodded. "You too."

Cullen watched Jacy and waited until she had driven far enough away from us that we could no longer hear her engine to turn his attention to me. "You two don't like the idea of your dad doing business with my dad, do you?"

I decided that giving Cullen no answer would probably be more in line with Dad's instructions about the Wheatleys than telling him the truth, so I stayed silent.

"It's pretty obvious how you feel," he said.

"I'm sorry," I said genuinely. "It's just that I like Back Trails the way it is."

"I don't blame you."

"You don't?"

"No. You've got a great life here. Once you start dealing with the kind of clients my dad can bring in for you, you'll be needing to take a vacation from your vacation paradise."

I laughed. "Pretty demanding?"

"Oh yeah." He squeezed his throttle a couple times to rev the engine but held it in neutral so that the machine couldn't move forward. "What I can't figure out is why your dad is even talking to my dad about it now. When Dad first contacted him last year, your dad was adamantly not interested."

"Wait. Your dad contacted my dad . . . last year?"

Cullen nodded. "Last year. And even though your dad basically said no way to his initial query, he scheduled this trip just to see the place in person. Dad figures he's pretty good at convincing people in person. When he can show guys the kind of money they can bring in, he almost always gets the deal he's after. He was planning on having to do quite a bit of convincing with your dad, but then he called Dad a week before we were due to leave asking my dad to put together a proposal after all."

"Hm." I scrounged my memory for something that might have happened in recent weeks to throw Dad into such a complete turnaround, but came up empty . . . except for the avalanche. But it had to be more than that. Avalanches happened every year, sometimes several times. And more often than not, the people getting killed in them were men. Men with kids at home. Why would this year's incident have impacted my father any differently than those in years past?

"I'll race you up." Cullen gave his machine full throttle and sped away from me up the groomed pass.

Who could ignore a challenge like that?

I put my machine in gear and drove faster than was probably reasonable or safe to catch him. And I did catch him. We drove along all the trails in the bottom of the valley and then started winding our way up the switchbacking trail to where people liked to high mark.

Avalanche country.

As I drove up and up ahead of Cullen on the narrowing trail, I could see all kinds of tracks and smudged snow where people had been attempting to go up slopes that were not part of the groomed trail network. I pointed them out to Cullen and then warned him by pointing three times down at the trail to not even think about following any one of them.

He stayed right behind me on the trail.

I drove more slowly as the elevation increased and pulled off the trail only to make room for snowmobilers coming down. They had the ledge side, and we had the slope side, so we were the ones who had to move out of the way. One snowmobiler in particular caught my attention, and I reached out to tug at her sleeve as she slowed down to creep by me. "Hey, Megan."

She smiled and lifted her left hand away from her hand brake to wave at me. "Hey."

"What are you doing up here alone?" The girl was new enough to the area that there was no way she could possibly know all the trails and landmarks yet.

She pulled off her dark goggles. "Dad's behind me. He's taking pictures for our website."

"Oh. Good."

"Headed up to see the avalanche site?"

"Yeah."

"Can hardly pick it out now," she said. "There's already a whole new overhang of snow on top."

"Ready and waiting for the next fool."

She nodded and put her goggles back on. "We're going to be on the trails all day," she said, "so maybe we'll pass each other again later."

"Sounds good. Just stay on the groomed trails, and you shouldn't have any problems."

"You're sweet, Dakota."

Cullen teased me about that when Megan had pulled away past us. Called me *sweet* and made little kissy noises. I tried to ignore him—to direct my intensity and focus into conquering the trail ahead instead of at all the stupid noise behind. I sped up for more engine noise and finally got enough ahead of him that his words no longer reached or bothered me.

What did bother me was his attitude once we pulled off to the side of the trail and killed our engines at the avalanche site. He wondered aloud if we mightn't find the buried body of the guy who'd died. He wondered aloud if it would be frozen solid and freezer burned like an unwrapped pork chop in a deep freeze. He wondered aloud if we couldn't be parked on top of it at this very moment.

I wondered silently whether he had any conscience at all.

To me the place felt as cold as it looked. White. Windswept. Barren. The thought that a man had lost his life here not nearly long enough ago to relegate it to at least the comfortable past chilled me even more than the brutal conditions.

"Let's get out of here," I said quietly to Cullen Wheatley. "I'll show you the Goose Lake trail. It's mainly National Forest, so you're allowed to ride around a little more. There're a couple lakes on it that freeze over solid."

But he seemed not to hear me. He was staring longingly up the slope.

CHAPTER 08

"Let's get out of here," I said again, loudly this time.

"Why?" Cullen challenged. "Are you afraid to drive up there?"

"Uh . . . yeah. And you would be too if you had a brain."

"I'm not afraid," he said.

Whether he was posturing or truly brainless enough to be serious, I didn't know—or care. I started my machine and drove a half circle in the snow to aim myself back down the mountain. If Cullen Wheatley wanted to kill himself, that was his business. I had no intention of being stuck anywhere near the path of his avalanche.

I'd driven nearly half a mile down the mountain without looking back before I heard his machine coming up behind mine. I had no idea whether or not he'd raced up the slope underneath the fresh overhang of snow. I didn't ask him either, and he didn't volunteer the information. We just drove to the Goose Lake Jeep Trail turnoff and headed into the trees toward Round Lake.

I smiled as I rode. The same six-mile stretch of road to Round Lake would take an hour on our ATVs during summer because of all the boulders, washouts, and slippery areas of loose rock and water. Three hours or so in an SUV if you were trying not to break anything. On snowmobiles Cullen and I made it to the lake in only minutes without even the slightest bump to slow our speed along the way.

At the lake Cullen and I drove full throttle back and forth and in circles over the ice, whose layers held us without groaning any complaint. I remembered the first time I'd been on Round Lake on a snowmobile. With Dad. When I was six. I'd enjoyed the ride until he'd told me it was a frozen-over lake we were riding on, and then I became fearful, sure we would break through and die. But we didn't. And I'd been on the lake loads of times in the years since without ever having any incident of anything other than great fun. It could be that Round Lake froze solid clear through to the bottom. I wasn't sure. But I was sure it would hold Cullen and me and anyone else who happened along for at least another month.

My father loved the speed he could achieve on the flat surface of the open ice. And spinning out when he pressed a certain way at his brake while going full speed. It was sort of an unspoken challenge he posed to himself. *How fast can I fly this machine and still be in split-second control if I needed to be? How wildly can I spin her and still be able to steer her straight again in an instant if I needed to?* Jacy always teased that he was like a little boy on his snowmobile when it was just us three without any clients along, and Dad always smiled and let her think that. But I knew differently. Little boys would spin out on purpose because it was fun, or to prove something to their buddies, or because they savored the thrill of surviving a couple of out-of-control moments. With Dad, it was all about control. Pushing limits and improving his ability all while staying in control of the machine and of his location on the ice in relation to everyone else on it.

I didn't like to spin out. On purpose or on accident. But I did like speed. I'd have been content to spend the rest of the afternoon at the lake just racing back and forth across it, but Cullen got bored after about ten minutes.

"What's further up?" he asked me when I pulled my machine alongside where he'd parked his back near the trail.

"More of the same."

Cullen looked thoughtful for a couple seconds. "Let's go check it out."

I shrugged and led the way further up the Goose Lake Trail. Beyond Round Lake, the snowmobile trails weren't groomed but were still marked by an occasional little orange strip painted on a tree. Plenty of ski tracks marked the snow, but it wasn't nearly as packed or smooth. Not a problem for the Wheatleys' machines though. It generally wasn't a problem for our machines either, except when we'd tried to come up once with clients who'd preferred to ride on our machines with us rather than drive their own. With the extra weight, the poor machines had just bogged down in the ten-foot-deep soft snow, especially along the sunny stretches of the trail where the snow had turned slushy. They could never quite get on top of it. But the Wheatleys' machines flew across it without difficulty. I suspected that they'd been purchased by the Wheatleys for this exact kind of riding. Cullen pulled out ahead of me and let out a whoop as if he'd finally encountered the snow he'd been destined to conquer.

We rode quite a ways up the trail before Cullen stopped and pointed at a track-covered slope across a small meadow from us. "Can we ride up that?"

I shook my head.

"It's in Wilderness Area?"

"No," I said. "It's legal to ride there. But it's dangerous."

"There's not an overhang like at the other place."

"There're still avalanches here. And this area is full of huge boulders. You can't see them now because of the snow, but you can sure see them in the summertime. Wouldn't want to hit one."

"There are tracks going up all over it," he said, pointing as if I couldn't see them for myself in the almost blinding white snow. "People have been doing it. We'll just stay in their tracks so we won't hit any buried boulders. It must be safe."

"It's always safe until it isn't," I said.

"That sounds like something my grandmother would say." Cullen laughed. "Little old lady." He revved his machine and then took off straight across the meadow and up the slope.

Nobody had ever called me *little old lady* before and it burned worse than frostbite, but I kept my snowmobile near the trail.

Cullen's machine maintained its rate of acceleration until the slope steepened sharply up. He pushed it through its sluggishness after that, standing nearly flat against it, and made it almost to the point where the snowmobiler who'd left the highest tracks had had to turn around before flipping his machine.

Almost. But the mark on the mountain was still higher than Cullen's.

Cullen turned his machine sideways across the slope, leaning all his weight into the mountain, and then settled in for the incredibly quick ride down and back across the meadow.

"Did you see how close I was?" he shouted to me as he sped toward me, stopping his machine short only inches away from mine. "If I start from a little further back and give it a little more power—"

"You could die young and leave a good-looking corpse," I said.

"Little old lady," he said, and took off again.

I watched him climb the slope and listened to him "Yeehaw" all the way down several times after that. Enough times to convince myself that the slope must indeed be safe and that there mustn't be any hidden boulders.

But not enough times for Cullen to ever surpass the previously set high mark.

"Little old lady," I called to him as I passed him going up as he came down.

The fear that my father, who was at home running numbers with Mr. Wheatley, would kill me himself if the mountain didn't did poke at the back part of my thinking. But I ignored it. I focused all my attention on my machine and on the goal just a little further up the slope.

The mountain rose up in front of me like a glaring white wall. I leaned into my machine, pushing it against the slope, and tried to ignore the ever-increasing pull of the huge emptiness behind me. The high mark was only a couple yards up. I could see it. And I could feel all of Cullen's failed attempts at reaching it underneath my machine as it sputtered over them and began to refuse my shouted and prayed commands to it.

I wasn't going to make it to the high mark.

As soon as I knew that, I leaned my side into the mountain, guided the machine through a quick choppy half turn, and then held on for life and limb as it sailed down steeply and quickly toward Cullen Wheatley and the flat meadow below.

What he said when he passed by me on his way up was no surprise, and it made me smile even as it turned my grip as hot as campfire coals around my handlebars. "Little old lady!"

CHAPTER 09

Cullen and I tried for nearly an hour to surpass that high mark, but never did. We never surpassed one another either. It seemed that our machines, which were exactly the same, would take us both, who were about the same size, to exactly the same point on the slope before threatening to quit. Maybe he'd gotten an inch or two higher than I had, or maybe I'd gotten an inch or two higher than he had, but there was really no way to tell in the mess of snow where we'd both always had to turn around. And anyway, an inch or two wasn't what either of us was looking for.

We wanted to beat each other by a yard.

And we wanted to pass the mark already there, even though it might have been made by a professional on a racing machine for all we knew. A more skilled driver. A more powerful, sleeker machine. Odds Cullen and I would never be able to beat, even by fluke. But on the unlikely chance that that high mark had been left by Joe Tourist from someplace where it never snowed on his luckiest day ever, we kept trying.

Cullen lost interest first. "Let's find our own place and make it just between you and me," he said. "That mark is distracting us."

I wanted to tell him all the reasons why that was a really bad idea.

I *knew* all the reasons why it was a really bad idea.

A different approach might affect the snow above differently.

A different approach might be strewn with snowed-over boulders.

A different approach might run onto a gaping hole or a vertical slope or an avalanche waiting to happen.

But I also knew that I did not want to be called *little old lady* again. And even more than that, I didn't want to *be* like a little old lady in Cullen's eyes or in my own.

"All right," I said.

We putted around awhile going back and forth along the section of trail in the valley in search of a slope that suited both of us. I would have preferred one that had tracks on it already, because that would have meant that at least one other person had gone up it and survived, but Cullen made it obnoxiously clear that he was looking for clean white pristine snow.

My insides tightened around something like fear, and I began to wish Dad was with us to either give me that "Do the right thing; be a man" look or else step in when I didn't have the courage to do the right thing and be a man for me. One way or the other, he'd get me out of this mess.

In the one moment when I figured I might be more afraid of dying than of being called a little old lady by Cullen Wheatley, I suggested to him that his father wouldn't be happy if we wrecked his machines.

"Ah," he said, waving away my comment like it was nothing more than a pesky insect, "a few thousand dollars is nothing to my dad. He'll just buy another one if he wants one."

"What if you wreck your neck and have to spend the rest of your life in a wheelchair?"

"I could do that staying home to be safe and slipping in my shower," he said. "You've got to live a little."

The problem was that I wanted to live a lot.

When Cullen thought he'd found the perfect slope for us, he slowed his machine beside mine and said, "Since I picked the slope, I'll go first. That way if anyone wrecks my dad's machine, it'll be me. And if anyone dies, it'll be me. Okay?"

"Okay," I said. "But are you sure you're ready to meet God?" I'd intended the question as not much more than a joke that one would make to someone who was about to do something stupid. But once the words were out of my mouth and hanging unanswered between us, I realized that this was actually the most legitimate and serious question I could ask someone who was about to do something stupid. So even though it was awkward and just plain out of the blue, I kept on. "Because I am. Although I don't know how much He'd appreciate having to let me meet Him early on account of my own stupidity."

"A time to be born, a time to die, right?" Cullen smiled. "Isn't that what the Bible says? Or a song or something? Anyway, if it isn't your time, you won't go."

"I'm serious, Cullen," I said. "Are you ready to meet God? Because I can tell you how to get ready."

After a couple seconds of tight silence, Cullen laughed. "God wouldn't want to meet me, Dakota," he said, and then sped away from me and straight up the slope he'd chosen.

I watched him and bit my lip.

His comment had surprised me. Here was a kid who had everything he could possibly want, except for maybe a decent family life. A kid for whom a few thousand dollars was nothing. Pocket change. A kid who could probably quite literally have anything he ever desired on this earth.

If he had said something like *I don't need God, Dakota,* or *You don't know anything I don't know,* or even *Only little old ladies worry about being ready to meet God, Dakota,* I wouldn't have been the slightest bit surprised. But *God wouldn't want to meet me, Dakota . . . ?*

Cullen sped up the slope as far as his whining machine would take him, spun her around, and came zipping down toward me. I watched the snow behind him to make sure it hadn't shifted or started moving. I followed his tracks up and down with my eyes to make sure they looked solidly continuous. Everything looked okay. Safe. So I tightened my hold on my handlebars, aimed my machine in the direction of the slope, and squeezed the throttle all the way against the handle.

"Little old lady!" Cullen and I shouted at one another at the same time as we passed by each other flying across the meadow.

I tried to follow Cullen's tracks up the slope exactly, but the loose fluffy snow yanked my machine into a course of its own. My skis made their own tracks just less than an inch to the left of Cullen's. When I reached the farthest point of where my machine would take me, well below Cullen's mark, I tried to spin her to the right as Cullen had, but she wouldn't go because of the steep sideways angle at which I'd been forced by the snow to come up. With all my strength, I pulled the machine to the left instead, making my own arc in the snow. I landed upright though I thought I might not, and started the descent.

You should always be in complete control, Dad's voice warned from my memory. And, *Don't follow someone into doing something wrong.*

I could see Cullen at the bottom of the meadow, standing on the seat of his snowmobile facing me and holding his right arm out straight to his side. Warning me to head to my left. I yanked the handlebars as firmly as I could in that direction, but the machine hit something just then and bounced to the right as if I were nothing more than a rag doll flopping around.

But I was not a rag doll.

I pressed all my weight backwards against my seat and gritted my teeth against the yanking of the snow on my skis. I wanted them to go one way; the snow wanted to pull them another. I could see the sudden drop-off, the hole, where the snow's route would eventually lead me, and I could see my one option for a safe—or at least not totally dangerous—ride down.

I had to make the machine go where *I* wanted it to go.

Even if that wasn't the way *it* wanted to go.

I held my breath.

Leaned into my handlebars. Forced them left.

They snapped back right, almost breaking my hold on them. I tried again to head the machine left.

I could see the drop-off right beside me.

Just ahead.

I held on to my machine as long as I could before it dipped forward and down, giving me my first full glimpse of the snow-coated rocky abyss I was plunging into. I immediately gave the machine throttle, trying to remember what I was supposed to do to save myself when plunging out of control into a ravine. The front end hit a sharp rock, dumping me first into the windshield and then hard onto the ground. I came down on snow and covered my eyes and head. The machine came down somewhere out ahead of me, bounced a couple times, and continued its noisy descent down the rest of the mountain.

I lay perfectly still. Hearing the machine crash against something and then something else. Hearing Cullen shouting. Hearing my own heart pounding in my ears.

Hearing Dad say again, *You should always be in complete control.*

And hearing myself whisper back to him, *Yes, sir.*

Knowing exactly what was coming.

The frightening silence. The even more frightening splintering sound. The deafening ground shaking, rumbling.

I rolled onto my left side and hurried to cover the side of my head with my right arm.

All I could see was snow.

I'm sorry, Dad.

I'm sorry, Lord.

Clouds of snow soared over me white and dark. Mounds of it fell on me. Buried me. Pinned my arm to my helmet. Snow jammed into the cracks of my helmet and settled cold on my face. My nose. My mouth. I couldn't move my legs or my head or my fingers. Its weight pressed on me, mercifully muffling the moan of the snow slide's roar. But then the snow beneath me began to shift and move too, and soon I and it and all the snow on top of us were rolling down the mountain in a frenzied noisy slide.

As I tumbled, I became more and more aware of pain.

Sometimes I couldn't see anything. Sometimes I could see the sky before another cloud of snow came down on top of me. Once I thought I saw a flash of silver metal. And then I saw only white that turned black as more white covered me.

I was on my side. Facing a boulder but not touching it. Snow covered me, but didn't fill in the space between my head and the rock, so I could breathe even though I couldn't move.

I lay there.

Unable to think about anything except the incredible weight of the white darkness all around me, and of how little air had been trapped between me and a boulder that could have killed me had I smacked into it.

I couldn't see.

I couldn't hear.

I couldn't pray.

I couldn't move.

I just lay there.

I didn't know if Cullen had been able to get out of the way of the snow or not before it collided with the meadow. I didn't know if he was buried somewhere too or looking for me. I didn't know if God would rescue me from an accident that had been the result of my own faulty choosing.

I didn't know if Dad would forgive me.

I did know I was getting cold.

Fast.

CHAPTER 11

"Dakota!"

Perfect clear sunlight filled the space between my face and the rock as two gloved hands shoveled away snow in handfuls. I realized then that the eye shield of my helmet was no longer intact.

"Dakota!"

"I'm all right," I muttered, even though I wasn't at all sure that I was. Melted snow dripped out the corner of my mouth.

"Lie still until I get all the snow off you," Cullen said. Commanded.

More melted snow dripped out of my mouth.

No, it couldn't be melted snow, because it was hot. And salty.

Blood.

Great.

"The heel of your boot was sticking out or I'd never have found you," Cullen said. He sounded almost frantic and out of breath with the work of unburying me.

"There're probe poles at Round Lake," I told him.

"Yeah," he said. "I saw them. But you'd have suffocated by the time I could get to them and get back with them and then find you."

"God is good," I said out loud. He had rescued me. He'd given me an air pocket. And He'd given Cullen a means of locating me. "Are you all right?" I asked Cullen.

"Yeah," he answered. "I pulled my machine back as soon as I saw what was happening and then tried to keep my eye on where you were. But it was just white. So much moving snow. I couldn't see anything until it started to settle."

"Snowblind," I said.

He leaned away from me. "You should be able to move now."

"I'm cold," I said.

"But can you move?"

I'd always been on the asking end of that question and not the one expected to answer. My body didn't want to move. In fact, what I really wanted to do was stay right where I was and go to sleep. But I knew enough to know that that was exactly what I needed to avoid doing. My legs felt as if wet sandbags had been strapped to them, but they did move. Slowly and with Cullen's assistance, I worked myself into a sitting position.

"Do you hurt anywhere?" Cullen was asking me.

"Nah . . ." I told him.

"Take a minute. Be sure."

I didn't need the full minute. "No. I think I'm okay."

Cullen got to his feet. "I've got to get you back to the house."

"Yeah," I said. It was hard to think clearly. "Is your dad's machine okay?"

Cullen shook his head. "I saw it come to pieces, and I'm sure it's buried down in the canyon somewhere."

"My dad's going to kill me," I muttered as I struggled to get to my feet in the choppy deep snow. "But, man, that was an awesome fall. I almost got by it, but—"

"Wish I'd had a video camera," Cullen said. "Here, let me help you."

"Please."

With my right arm over Cullen's shoulders and his left arm around my waist, the two of us climbed out of the snow mound I'd been buried in and picked our way back to Cullen's snowmobile.

Once I was sitting on the seat behind him and had caught my breath, I asked Cullen if he figured we should look for his father's machine.

"We can come back for it," he said. "It's not like it's going to go anywhere." He started his machine and drove us out of there. The snowmobile didn't bog or complain at all about being expected to carry two of us through the deep snow on the ungroomed part of the trail. It managed the task far better than any of our machines would have.

By the time we arrived back at the house, my body was letting me know all too loudly and clearly that it did not appreciate being thrown off a snowmobile and tumbling down into a ravine. I'd have bumps and bruises for sure, though I'd escaped the accident—incident—with no broken bones.

Cullen left me on the seat and ran up the stairs and inside. I thought for a moment about staying put and waiting for someone to come help me since my legs felt so numb and heavy that the stairs might as well have been Mt. Everest. But I suspected things would go easier with Dad if I showed up in the house on my own two feet.

He'd take me inside. Start me on getting warmed back up. He'd tell me I'd been stupid but that he was glad I was okay, and that I'd have to work like a pack horse for the next several months in order to earn enough money from him and anyone else who'd hire me to repay Mr. Wheatley for his machine—whether or not Mr. Wheatley needed or wanted the money.

And I'd be glad to hear it too. Even if Dad followed it up by announcing that he and Mr. Wheatley had formed a partnership and that as of next winter Back Trails would no longer be Back

Trails but Rolling Meadows Snow Chateau . . . or something like that.

Dad and I met at the front door. He stepped back. I stepped past him.

And came face to face with Mr. Wheatley.

"I wrecked your machine, sir," I whispered to him because that's all the voice I had. "But I'll pay for it. I will."

"That can wait," Dad said behind me, "until after I've had a good look at you and have made sure you're not more hurt than Cullen says you think you are."

Mr. Wheatley nodded. "Of course."

Dad shut the heavy wood front door.

The stiff sound of it and of my father's too-steady calmness unnerved me as he helped me get out of my wet snow gear, asked me questions about the wreck, and pressed at my back and mid-section.

More than the fact that I might have been killed.

More than the fact that I'd wrecked a several-thousand-dollar snowmobile.

Dad stood up, held his hand on my shoulder for a long couple seconds while he told Jacy to heat some water for hot chocolate. Then he looked at me again. "Looks like everything's where it's supposed to be, Dakota, but you tell me right away if you start having pain anywhere."

I nodded. *Yes, sir.*

"Come on," he said, grabbing hold of my arm, "let's get you comfortable."

"I'll get a couple of blankets," Amberlee volunteered.

Dad thanked her.

"Mr. Craig," Cullen began, but looked down and stopped talking when Dad turned to face him.

Dad waited through as much icy silence as he'd ever been likely to tolerate, which wasn't much. Then he tightened his hold on my arm and walked with me to the chair nearest the wood stove.

CHAPTER 12

"Running!" I shouted in response to Dad's stick figure drawing with one leg forward, one leg back, one arm forward, one arm back. After a good night's sleep and a whole day of sitting around doing nothing but schoolwork and thinking about how stupid I'd been, I was glad for the distraction of a good game of "Draw and Guess"—Craig vs. Wheatley. "Runner. Jogger. Olympics."

Across the coffee table from Dad and Jacy and me, Amberlee and Cullen were shouting out similar things in their attempt to guess the correct word from their father's drawing. "Race. Racer. Track and field. Cross country."

Dad scribbled another stick figure sketch of a guy chopping wood.

I called out, "Exercise!" and Dad whispered "Yes!" while Mr. Wheatley dropped his pencil and shook his head.

Next it was Cullen's and my turn to draw. I lifted the closed dictionary from the middle of the table and handed it across to Cullen. "You choose the word."

He wrote one on a slip of paper and handed it to me. "Do you know what that is?"

Easy for him to ask since he had the definition sitting right there in front of him. "I think so," I told him. It wasn't a word Dad, Jace, or I used every day, but the Wheatleys needed to get a point on the board anyway. The score so far was 6-0.

When Jacy flipped the timer over, I drew a mountain, a stick figure guy on skis, and a cable above the slope with one of those little cars suspended from it.

"Ski resort," Jacy said.

"Ski resort?" Cullen glanced over at my picture, and while he did I took a look at his. He'd drawn a boat and a guy playing a violin.

I circled the little car hanging from the cable in my picture.

"Ski lift?" Jacy asked.

"Venice," Mr. Wheatley said.

Cullen moved his hand to signal his father to keep guessing in that direction.

I pointed at the little car again with the tip of my pencil and looked at Dad.

"Oh," he said, "what is that thing called?"

"Canal," Mr. Wheatley said. "Serenade."

No doubt the Wheatleys would win this point if Cullen would circle his little boat the way I'd circled my little car, but he didn't do that. He just kept pointing at his picture.

"I've been in one of those things," Dad said. "They run them over the ski slopes in the summer for mountain bikers."

"Gondola!" Jacy shouted. "Right?"

"You got it," I said. "Good job."

Mr. Wheatley leaned back in frustration. "I think this is a lost cause. We're never going to score against you people."

"That's because these people know each other well enough to know how the others think." Amberlee stood up, dropped the pillow she'd been hugging back into its corner of the couch, and stomped her way to the kitchen.

Dad glanced questioningly at Mr. Wheatley.

The man shrugged in response. "She doesn't like to lose."

Jacy started gathering pencils and scraps of paper. Apparently the game was over.

I decided to go console Amberlee. Dad and Jacy and I almost always won when we played a game as a team. Any game. But when I walked into the kitchen to find Amberlee standing in front of the sink crying, I wished I'd left the task of consoling to my sister—or better yet to her own father or brother. Even though she turned her back to me when she saw me, I didn't feel like walking away would be the right thing to do.

"Hey," I said quietly, not stepping toward her, "it's just a game. Your dad almost got that last one."

"It's not the game, Dakota," she said.

Obviously. I rubbed the back of my ear and looked down at the floor.

Slowly, after wiping at her eyes with the backs of her hands, Amberlee turned to face me. "Thanks for caring though. That's more than my dad ever does."

This was none of my business. And way beyond what I'd bargained for when I'd set out to cheer her up. "Amberlee—"

"You're lucky to be so close to your dad."

"We spend a lot of time together," was all I could think to say since I certainly hadn't felt particularly close to Dad during the Wheatleys' stay at Back Trails.

"My dad has no idea who I am," Amberlee went on. "He doesn't know I play the flute or that I want to be a paramedic or that—"

"You want to be a paramedic?"

She nodded. "I've already started taking courses. My dad doesn't know that either. And even worse than his not knowing is that I don't think he'd care even if he did know."

"I'm sure that's not true," I said. "You ought to tell him and give him the chance to care."

"Yeah." She laughed coldly. "When? A PS on the bottom of his Christmas card?"

"Well . . . what are you doing tomorrow? You could ask him to take you snowmobiling."

"I hate snowmobiling, Dak—"

"Just the two of you. And when you stop to eat the lunch you packed ahead of time, you two could talk." I expected her to scoff again. When she didn't, I added, "Give him a chance. He might be just as afraid as you are."

"Afraid?"

"Yeah. You know, that you don't care about him."

"And what if he's not?" she asked. "What if he's just a jerk like Mom always says he is?"

How should I know what if then? was what I thought. But I said, "Then at least you'd have given him the chance, and you'll know for sure."

She stayed quiet for several seconds.

So did I. There was no way I wanted to say anything else and open up another round of tough—and none of my business anyway—questions.

When Jacy came in the kitchen to cut Cullen and Mr. Wheatley each a piece of apple pie, I muttered something about my sore back and made my escape. I hated getting into murky personal conversations with clients, and especially girl clients. I figured that people ought to be able to leave their unresolved issues at home when they went on vacation.

Of course the Wheatleys weren't on vacation—a fact that fuelled a hefty unresolved issue of my own.

CHAPTER 13

My back hurt the next morning. So did my left knee. And my right shoulder. I lay in bed as long as I could stand it, but then as soon as it started getting light I got up. I might as well head downstairs to take some painkillers and start breakfast. I could whip together a truly fine western omelet when I set my mind to it. My physical discomfort definitely warranted my setting my mind to something else. Anything else.

I was surprised to find the light already on in the kitchen, and even more surprised to find Amberlee Wheatley standing at the counter making sandwiches.

Good thing I'd decided to get showered and dressed first instead of coming down in my pajamas like I usually would have this early in the morning. I'd hoped that the hot shower might soothe my back and shoulder, but it hadn't.

"Morning," I said to Amberlee. "You're up early."

"My dad and I are going snowmobiling today," she said. "I asked him if he'd like to take me, like you said, and he said he'd love to."

"Good," I said.

"Cullen invited himself to come along," she said, frowning a little for the first time, "but that's okay. He'll probably want to ride around all day, so Dad and I should still get in some talk time alone."

I shuddered. "Just don't let him go high marking."

Amberlee smiled. "Hopefully he's smart enough to not want to after watching you get buried by half a mountain."

"It wasn't half a mountain."

"You're so cute." She went back to her sandwich making.

"You'll probably have to use one of our machines on account of—"

"I'm going to ride with my dad on his . . . well, you were on his . . . but on the one he's riding."

I took the bottle of painkillers from the cupboard above the stove. "I hope the day goes well for you guys. I really do."

"Thanks," Amberlee said. "So do I."

Dad came into the kitchen carrying a leather portfolio, a set of keys, and a packed overnight bag. He muttered "Morning" to Amberlee, nodded at me, and then grabbed the bottle of painkillers out of my hand before I'd even had a chance to open it.

"You all right, Dad?" I asked him. "Where are you going?"

"Headache," he said. "Billings."

"Billings?"

He nodded. "I'm going to show Wheatley's proposal to Sam and see what he thinks."

Sam Tescher. Dad's attorney.

"Can't you just call him?"

Frustrated with the childproof bottle cap that he was having a hard time opening and with me, Dad shook his head.

"Let me get that for you, Dad," I said carefully. "I need some anyway. My shoulder's really bugging me this morning." It had been a long time since Dad had gotten one of his bad headaches, and I'd almost forgotten how irritable he could become during one.

He handed the bottle back to me without a word.

On her way back to the sink after putting the mustard away in the refrigerator, Amberlee stopped and looked closely at Dad.

"Are you sure it's just a headache, Mr. Craig?" she asked him. "You really don't look well."

"Just need to get the edge off," Dad told her as he took the three tablets I held out to him, "then I'll be fine."

Amberlee reached up to touch his forehead, but Dad moved quickly away from her hand. "I've talked to your sister already," he said to me. "I should be back tomorrow at the latest. You two can handle things around here?"

"Yeah," I said. "Sure." I was about to walk away when I remembered what I'd told Amberlee Wheatley just the day before. *You ought to talk to your dad. Give him a chance. He might be just as afraid as you are.* Then I remembered Jacy urging me to talk to Dad about why he'd called the Wheatleys and why he suddenly wanted to do something different with Back Trails. *You should talk to him, Dakota. Man to man.*

Dad intended to drive to Billings to speak with his attorney about Mr. Wheatley's proposal. If I didn't try to talk to him now, he might make his decision there, and then whatever I might say later wouldn't matter anyway.

"Dad," I ventured, "do you want some company? That way if your headache doesn't let up, you could sleep and I could drive."

I fully expected Dad to reject the suggestion right away, but he didn't.

So I ventured a little further. "And maybe, you know, we could talk about this a little more. You and me."

I watched my father's face for a clue to what his response would be before he spoke it. Amberlee was right. He did not look well. He looked like he couldn't even think clearly.

"That might be good," he said finally. "All right. I'll go tell your sister. You go pack some gear since we'll have to spend the night."

Dad left Jacy with a long hug and a short list of instructions. I left her with the promise that I'd do my best to get him to talk to me about what was really going on with him regarding Back Trails. The two of us rode snowmobiles out of Cooke Pass toward the top of the Chief Joseph Scenic Highway, which they kept plowed to the Beartooth Highway. Dad always parked one of our green Back Trails SUVs up there for the winter just in case we ever needed to head more quickly to Billings over Dead Indian Hill than we could get there taking the long route through the Park and back around.

As I followed my father along turn after turn on the unplowed highway, I wished he'd go faster. I suspected he was thinking I might be a little wary on a snowmobile considering what had happened to me the last time I'd been on one, but I was much more anxious about the several hours we'd be together during the drive to Billings and wanted to get that started and over with as quickly as possible. I hoped he would talk to me about Back Trails, but if he made up his mind not to, it could be a long and stiffly uncomfortable trip.

When Dad slowed down even more in front of me and finally came to a complete stop, I concluded that something must be wrong with his machine. But leaving it running, he climbed off and ran down the slope to the right of the road and into a thick of trees where he leaned forward with his hands on his knees and threw up on the ground.

I got off my machine and made my way slowly through the waist-deep snow and down the slippery bank toward him. I wanted to give him plenty of time to steady himself but still wanted to be there to help him climb back up to the highway if he was feeling weak or dizzy.

I couldn't remember a time when he'd had a headache severe enough to make him vomit, though I did know that that could happen.

I met Dad near the bottom of the slope and took hold of his arm.

He didn't pull away.

"I'm sorry," he said.

"Must be some headache," I said.

"There's something I haven't told you," he said.

I stopped walking and waited for him to look at me.

He didn't. "Let's get to the SUV first," he said. "It's cold out here."

Dad slept. I drove.

The wet two-lane highway stretched out ahead of me between mounds of bright white snow and underneath a dull white sky. I had believed that I'd feel better once I knew what had flung my father into his urgent rush to make Back Trails more secure. I had believed that knowing would make me feel more in control somehow. Less angry.

But now that he had told me, I knew that there were worse things than feeling powerless or angry.

Like feeling scared.

"I'd been hoping," Dad had told me slowly once we'd finally gotten the SUV dug out of a snowdrift, started, warmed up, and on the road, "to put off having this conversation until I had some kind of definite information for you and your sister." Dad had been driving then, and his hands had gone tight around the steering wheel. "But maybe it's better this way. I don't know. I sure wouldn't have had the energy to dig the outfit out without your help. I do know that."

"What's going on, Dad?"

For just an instant he'd looked at me then. Eye to eye before turning his attention back to the road. Almost as if he was waiting for permission from me.

Permission I wasn't at all sure I wanted to give him.

"Along with seeing Sam in Billings today," he'd begun, "I'm going to see a specialist about the results of some tests."

"Tests?"

He'd then explained that when he'd left Jace and me alone at the house a couple weeks earlier to drive some clients out through the Park, he'd stopped in at a clinic because he still wasn't feeling right after having the flu. They'd given him some blood tests to determine whether or not he'd come into contact with some kind of virus. No. Since traveling back and forth would be an issue for us, they'd decided then to check for other things because the first tests had shown elevated transaminases—whatever that meant—and high bilirubin. Definitely something with the liver, they'd told him, but the options outside of viral hepatitis, which his blood work had shown no markers for, were not good. Cancer. Cirrhosis. An autoimmune condition. They'd sent those tests on to the doctor in Billings we'd be going to see when we got there that afternoon.

"So," Dad had finished, "I'm just hoping he'll be able to tell me something I'm going to want to hear."

"Why didn't you tell us right away?" I'd asked him. "We could have been there for you. Helped you more. I don't know. But you shouldn't have kept this from us."

"I didn't want you and Jacy to be afraid over something that might turn out to be nothing. After the way your mother died and all."

Mom had died from what had started as a simple flu virus. Jacy, who'd been old enough when that had happened to remember it now, would definitely not respond well to this news.

"I guess I can understand your thinking," I'd said after a long half mile.

Then when we'd been on the road for an hour or so without a whole lot more talking, Dad had asked me if I'd mind driving. We'd pulled over to switch seats, and Dad had been asleep ever since.

Everything made more sense now.

Dad's phone call to the Wheatleys.

His staying home from church Sunday morning.

His asking me to keep the wood stove going at night even though he was home.

His strange poor color the day I'd run into him on Republic Pass.

But the fact that things made more sense provided about as much comfort as a pair of drenched gloves.

I drove us all the way to Billings and into downtown before waking Dad. "Where to?" I needed to know.

"Doctor's office first," he answered. "Then Sam's. And we're going to go to Pastor Adams's place for the night."

I nodded. Seeing Pastor Adams would be good. "Are you feeling any better?"

"I'm all right."

"Do you want to stop and eat or anything first?"

He shook his head. "But if you're hungry, pull into a drive-through and grab something."

I wasn't hungry. "So do you just . . . feel sick all the time?"

"Not all the time."

"I wish I'd known. I mean, I understand why you didn't tell us, but I wish I'd known before now."

"Why?" Dad kept looking out his side window. "So we could have spent the whole past two weeks like this? Not knowing what to say to each other?"

"I haven't known what to say to you for the past few days anyway."

"There's nothing *to* say," he said. "At least until we know what it is we need to be talking about."

"There's plenty to say," I said.

"So say it."

I could *think* of a million things I wanted my father to know. I loved him. I loved our life up in Cooke Pass. I'd be happy to stay there doing what we do forever. I didn't like the Wheatleys, but when I'd seen Amberlee crying, I'd felt sorry for her. I didn't want him to change Back Trails. I felt angry and ashamed at the same time that he hadn't felt secure enough in my ability to handle this situation to trust me to help him through it.

But thinking and saying were two different things.

So I settled on something safe. Well, maybe not safe. But something I'd have to say eventually anyway. "I'm sorry I wrecked Mr. Wheatley's machine. I will pay for it. Or pay you back for it after you pay for it. Whatever."

Dad nodded. "You told me about the actual wreck. I want to know what led up to it. What led up to your thinking high marking was going to be a good idea."

I told him.

Cullen's teasing.

My being angry that he'd stayed home from church to run numbers with Mr. Wheatley.

"I'm sorry," he said. "And you know what else?"

"What?"

He laughed a little as he rubbed at his temples with the heels of his hands. "We never did get those numbers run. Sunday morning was a rough one."

"Like this morning?"

He nodded.

"Dad," I said, willing to risk some flat-out take-it-for-what-it's-worth honesty since he had, "you know how I feel about Back Trails. I don't want it to change, at least not the way Mr. Wheatley is proposing we change it." It amazed me as I spoke how much easier it was to talk about the business with Dad now that the business was really the least of my concerns.

"I will take that into consideration," Dad said. Then much more quietly, he added, "Guys don't typically get up and walk away from wrecks like that. I'm glad you're okay, Dakota."

I prayed I'd be able to say the same thing to him when all his test results were in.

CHAPTER 15

"So this illness is why you've been looking to make changes to Back Trails?" Pastor Bruce Adams asked Dad. The three of us had just finished cleaning up his kitchen after dinner —a dinner that Dad had hardly touched—and had sat down in his front room to talk awhile.

Dad had met Pastor Adams a couple of years earlier during a river rafting trip in Idaho. The two of them had become almost instant friends, mainly because both of them had lost their wives and could relate to one another's grief. Pastor Adams had come to Back Trails twice since then as a client. Once with his son Ezra who was now away at college, and once with his church youth group. Both of those visits had turned into adventures for Dad and Jacy and me. Adventures that had drawn first Jacy, then me, and finally Dad to God.

Pastor Adams had become our Christian role model and mentor and was one of the few people my father trusted.

"Yeah, Bruce," Dad said. "I want things to be secure for the kids if . . ." He didn't finish.

"And you think the offer you have before you now is the right one?"

Dad blew air out through his lips. "It's the only one."

"Your lawyer says it looks sound?"

"Yeah."

"Are you convinced it's what God wants?"

"God?" Dad squinted at his friend. "Let's get real, Bruce. If I die, God's not going to come down and take care of things for my kids. And if I'm going to be sick for a long time, I don't want them having to worry about figuring out what to do with the business on top of worrying about taking care of me." He leaned forward in his chair.

"If," Pastor Adams said, "if, if. Hayden, you can't make decisions based on *if*. You've got to be able to see where you're coming from and where you're headed before you make decisions. Have you asked God what He'd have you do?"

"Yeah, I've prayed," Dad said.

"And this is His answer? This thing with Wheatley?"

"I don't have an answer, Bruce. He didn't give me any answers. So I'm just doing what I think needs to be done."

"Helping Him along a little?"

Both men were leaning forward now with their elbows on their knees.

"Hayden, for yourself and for your kids," Pastor Adams said, "and for God, wait for your test results before you make any decisions about the business or anything else. Do you remember what happened when Abraham tried to help God along? We're still seeing the consequences of that decision thousands of years later."

I didn't have a clue what Abraham had done to help God along or what consequences we were still seeing to this day because of it, but Dad seemed to. He nodded anyway.

"Bruce," he said, "I've tried to pray about it and to think about what would be pleasing to God. But I don't know enough to know what He would want me to do. And I don't even know how He'd tell me."

"You've only been a Christian for six months," Pastor Adams said. "Knowing like that comes with time. Time spent communing with God in prayer. Time spent reading and studying the

Bible. Time spent learning from people who've known Him longer than you have."

"The Bible says something about who I should go into business with?"

Dad's question, though asked with a tinge of sarcasm, was sincere, and Pastor Adams responded to it instantly. "The Bible says we shouldn't be unequally yoked together with unbelievers. People apply that to marriage most frequently, but I believe it also applies to business and any other close association. What happens if you put a big strong ox in the same yoke as a young weak one?"

"They won't go the same speed, and the cart or plow or whatever will just go in circles and eventually upset."

"Exactly," Pastor Adams said. "If you, a believer, go into business with Trevor Wheatley, who is . . . ?"

"Not a believer," Dad said. "I asked him outright."

"He's going to want to take the business places and in directions that you're not going to want to take it."

"Like selling alcohol."

"Yes," Pastor Adams said. "Like selling alcohol."

"I never did feel right about that," Dad confessed.

"And maybe that was God trying to tell you what He wants, or in this case something He doesn't want, for your business."

"But Bruce," Dad said, "when Jacy and Dakota go off to school and get part-time jobs at pizza places or whatever, they're going to be working with nonbelievers. That's just the way it is."

"Yes. And we have to be in the world in order to be lights in the world. But in things like our marriage or our own business or our closest friendships, we need to make the choice to follow the Bible's directive. It's for our own good. It protects us from being put in the position of having to make compromising choices and tends to leave us freer to serve God the way we ought to."

Dad said he understood.

Pastor Adams said the Bible has the answer for everything. It's just a matter of learning what the Bible says so you can apply it when life's questions arise. Then he said, "So tell me everything the doctor said when you saw him this afternoon."

Defeat showed in Dad's expression when he leaned back in his chair to answer. "Basically nothing. The test results are inconclusive so far. I've got to go back tomorrow morning for some more tests, and maybe then he'll know something . . . after a few more days."

"Sometimes," the pastor said as he stood up, "the waiting is tougher than the finding out. You guys feel like doing something to get your minds off it for a while? A little shopping maybe, since you're in Billings? I could give Will a call. Maybe he and Taren would be free to come with us."

We'd met Will Benjamin and his daughter Taren last August when they'd come to Back Trails with Pastor Adams's youth group for a six-day backpacking trip to the Sky Top Lakes. During that trip, Mr. Benjamin had saved Jacy's life when she'd slid down a glacier and into the frigid melt-off below. I thought it would be great to see him again. And his daughter Taren. But I left it to Dad to answer for us. He might not feel up to shopping. Or to a bunch of visiting.

He answered slowly. "I'm pretty tired, Bruce. But there are a few things we could use to get ready for the summer." He looked at me. "If I make a list, do you mind picking them up?"

It wasn't the shopping I would mind. It was the being away from Dad right then. But I didn't know how to say that without sounding stupid, so I told him I'd get the stuff. No problem.

Nobody answered at the Benjamins' house when Pastor Adams tried calling them, so he and I headed alone to the west end of town where there were several sporting goods stores. On the way Pastor Adams filled me in on everything that had been happening in his church, with his son Ezra, and with the Benjamins. After hearing the news that Taren's parents had indeed remarried, and that the whole family was actively involved at Pastor Adams's church, and that Mr. Benjamin had gotten a job with the Yellowstone County sheriff's department, I vowed to myself to try to do better at keeping in touch with people once they left Back Trails. Especially people like Mr. Benjamin.

Shopping did turn out to be a decent enough distraction, at least for a little while, and I found all the items on Dad's list at far better prices than we could ever have hoped to find them in Cooke City or when we came back to Billings at the end of spring to stock up for the summer. Two new tents. Four pairs of wick-dry hiking socks. A new camp lantern. And several cartons of vacuum-sealed backpacking food.

"The lantern's in case we can't have campfires again this year," I told Pastor Adams on the way back to his house,—as if he needed it explained—"and we need food for eight full hikes."

A full hike was a five-to-seven-day hike with our maximum of fifteen people, twelve clients and Dad, Jacy, and me. We were scheduled solid already for the upcoming summer. In fact, Dad had been forced for the first time since starting Back Trails to turn clients away because there simply were not enough weeks between snowmelt and snowfall to safely accommodate them with even the hope of decent weather.

"It's cruel," I said to Pastor Adams when he killed his engine in his driveway and the two of us sat there in the darkness without moving to get out of his truck, "that one week things can seem to be cruising just fine and the next week everything seems to be crashing."

I half-expected him to seize on the *cruising* and *crashing* aspect of my comment to turn my recent snowmobiling incident into a life lesson somehow. Maybe because my first thought once the words had come out of my mouth was *Sort of like your snowmobile, eh, Dakota?*

But he didn't. "Life is cruel sometimes," he said. "We live in a fallen world, and being Christians doesn't immunize us from its perils. But God—"

I didn't want to be rude. Especially to Pastor Adams. But I wanted even less to hear about God being good or in control. So I pushed open my door, filling the cab of the truck with warm light from above our heads and cold air from outside.

"I'll get your gear." Pastor Adams squeezed my shoulder before pushing open his own door and tossing his key ring across the empty middle seat to me. "You go check on your dad."

I nodded, relieved he'd understood.

CHAPTER 16

Dad and I arrived back at our house Wednesday afternoon to find Mr. Wheatley sitting at our dining room table with all of Dad's financial records from the previous few years spread out in neat little stacks.

"I see you've been making yourself at home, Trevor," Dad commented with surprising calmness. "Where's Jacy?"

"She took Cullen and Amberlee to Cooke City for lunch." Mr. Wheatley picked up the papers that were immediately in front of him and tapped them against the table until they straightened themselves into a tidy stack. "I took the liberty of looking over your records, and I think . . ." He set the papers down and stood to approach Dad. "I think I'm prepared to make you an offer for Back Trails that you'd be a fool to refuse."

"Different from the one you already gave me? My lawyer—"

"Better than the one I already gave you."

I stood speechless beside my father. I didn't think I'd ever met a man with more nerve. More arrogance. More audacity. More . . . I didn't even know a word that described whatever it was that Mr. Wheatley possessed that made him figure he had the right to go through another man's personal records without being invited to do so for the sake of business.

I prepared myself to physically hold my father back. Or to at least try to.

"So let's hear it," Dad said, standing perfectly still beside me. He didn't fold his arms across his chest or shove his hands into his pockets. He just stood there.

"I'm really not interested," Mr. Wheatley said, "in the kind of clients you've previously been entertaining. I'm looking for a more sophisticated traveler. Not hikers and hunters and youth groups. And I don't think you are cut out to cater to the needs of the kind of client I'm going to be bringing in instead." He found a pen underneath one of his stacks of Dad's papers and scribbled a few numbers onto the back of a receipt. He looked at it for a moment, conspicuously added another zero, and held it out across the table toward Dad. "I'd like to buy you out outright. How does that number suit you?"

Dad glanced quickly at the number Mr. Wheatley had scrawled onto the back of the receipt. A receipt for elk scent, I couldn't help noticing backwards through the thin paper as I deliberately avoided looking at Mr. Wheatley's offer.

That was Dad's business. Not mine.

"Hm," Dad said. "I could retire nicely on that."

Mr. Wheatley nodded. "Never have to work again."

"What do you think?"

It took me a moment to realize that Dad had directed that question at me. He held the receipt out in the open in front of me and tapped the number written there with his thumb.

"Look like a reasonable offer to you, son?"

I counted the zeros behind the first two numbers twice.

"I took off a few thousand for that snowmobile, of course," Mr. Wheatley said.

Of course.

Mr. Wheatley reached to grab one of his stacks of Dad's papers, but Dad raised his hand to stop him.

"I'll thank you not to touch those again," he said. Then he held the receipt out across the table. "This offer is intriguing,

Trevor, but my son and I have come to a kind of unspoken understanding."

I felt obligated somehow to interrupt him. "Dad, if you want to—"

"Back Trails is going to stay Back Trails," Dad told Mr. Wheatley, assuring me without even having to look at me. "And it's going to stay in the Craig family. No matter what."

There wasn't much for the two men to discuss after that. Dad got busy putting his financial records back into the clear plastic tote where they belonged, while Mr. Wheatley got busy loading his calculator and other business paraphernalia back into his briefcase.

"Oh," Dad said suddenly, "one more thing." He left the dining room, stayed in his office for a couple minutes, and returned with a folded check for Mr. Wheatley. "I think you'll find that adequate to replace your machine," he said. Then he laughed a little. Coldly. "And I guess you know I'm good for it."

Mr. Wheatley looked at the check, nodded, and slid it into his shirt pocket. "I guess you'll be wanting the kids and me to leave now?"

"You're reserved through Saturday," Dad answered, "and you're still welcome to it. But I haven't been feeling all that well, Trevor, and I don't think I'll be up to taking you—"

"I'm not looking so much to do stuff with the kids, Hayden," Mr. Wheatley said. "That's all we ever do. Do stuff. I'm just looking to be with them. And if we take off out of here now and head home, that probably won't happen. At least not this year."

"Make yourself at home," Dad said. He glanced at the dining room table, still covered with his financial records. "Except for in my office."

Mr. Wheatley nodded, looking uncomfortable for the first time since I'd met him. When he'd stood there for a couple minutes without knowing what to say, he nodded again, picked up his briefcase, and left the room.

"It's nice of you to let him stay," I said to Dad.

"Well, I could use the money," he said. Then he grinned and lightly smacked the top of my head with a stack of bank statements folded in thirds. "You cost me a lot this week."

He was teasing and I knew it, but the comment still stung. Not because he'd said it, but because it was true. I waited for him to finish twisting a rubber band around his stack of bank statements. "I really am sorry, Dad."

"I know you are." He dropped his bundle of statements into the open tote at his feet. "We'll work off the cost of Wheatley's machine the same way we're going to work off your speeding fine. It'll save us money in the long run because you're a better worker than any of the guys I've hired on before. And hey," he paused to grin and took a good long moment to enjoy it, "it's eighty pounds off my back for those climbs up the back side of Granite Peak, so I'll be whistling happy with the arrangement."

I smiled too and poked a couple times at his belly. "Not afraid of getting a little out of shape? You know, you're right at that age. Less work, more waist."

"I'll stay in plenty good shape keeping you moving at a decent pace," he said. "Don't you worry about me."

Don't you worry about me.

The statement dropped between us like a cloud of toxic air. Dad stepped away from it first, back to sorting his papers. After a moment, I joined him.

The doctor would be calling within a few days to let him know the results of the tests they'd run in Billings. Until then, we could only wait and try not to think about the worst-case scenarios.

Unfortunately, those seemed to be the ones that came most frequently and powerfully to mind.

CHAPTER 17

As soon as Jacy returned home with Cullen and Amberlee, Dad invited her to come and have a look at the things I'd bought in Billings and maybe help him put them away. Figuring they'd be in the supply room for quite a while, I made myself comfortable on the chair next to the woodstove and prayed that, for Dad's sake, he'd be able to tell her what was going on with him without her panicking or crying or any of that other girly emotional stuff. Dad needed us to be strong for him and would need that even more if the doctor called with bad news.

"How was Billings?" Amberlee Wheatley sat in the chair closest to mine and held a bowl of popcorn toward me.

I took a small handful. "It wasn't our best trip there," I said. "How was your snowmobiling ride with your dad?"

"I think it *might* have been the best trip we've ever had."

"I'm glad."

"I heard your dad turned down my dad's offer."

I nodded.

"That doesn't surprise me," she said. "I wouldn't want to change this place either." She grinned. "Well, it could use some new furniture and maybe a hot tub somewhere on the premises, but I like the rustic feel and pace of the place just like it is."

"Is your dad disappointed?"

She offered me another go at the popcorn. When I shook my head, she said, "I don't think so. To tell you the truth, I think he's happy to have a few more days here without having to think about proposals and numbers and all that anymore. I suppose your dad's relieved to not have to think about that stuff anymore too."

"He's got plenty on his mind without it," I said.

"Is he feeling better?" Her expression went serious as she set the bowl of popcorn on the coffee table. "He really didn't look good yesterday at all."

"Is that the future paramedic talking?"

Amberlee smiled down at her knees. "Maybe."

"He's pretty sick," I told her. And then I explained. If nothing else, it would keep her from bugging Dad to take her snowshoeing or skiing or asking him when he planned to make lunch.

"Wow," she said. "I had no idea."

"Neither did I until yesterday."

"Well . . . you believe in God, right?"

"Yeah."

"Pray it's just hepatitis A," she said. "That goes away by itself. I think."

I shook my head. "They tested for that already, and it's not that."

She leaned forward with her elbow on her knee and tapped her fingertips against her pursed lips.

I hoped they'd teach Amberlee some *Attempt to Keep Your Face from Revealing Your True Hopelessness* classes at her paramedic school, because she'd sure need to work on that for the sake of her future patients' loved ones.

"Can I use your computer?" She practically jumped to her feet.

"Yeah. Sure. It's in Dad's office."

"I'm going to do some research. Maybe there's something we can do to lessen your dad's symptoms and make him more comfortable."

I recognized that Amberlee was trying to be helpful. But the words she'd chosen made me cold. Didn't people only talk about making people more comfortable when they thought they were just waiting for them to die?

Like a run-over dog on the way to the vet to be put to sleep . . . or out to the woods to be shot.

I decided to get up and go look for Cullen. I found him in the dining room working at a crossword puzzle in the *Billings Gazette* that Pastor Adams had sent home with Dad and me.

"King," I said, looking over his shoulder. "Six down. A four-letter word for 'queen's husband.' "

Cullen wrote it in. "Thanks. Now maybe you'd like to help me with some of the hard ones?"

I pulled out a chair and sat down. "Not really."

"I was thinking," he said, "that it would be really fun to come back up here in the summer so we could ride some of those trails we rode on ATVs."

I shoved his left shoulder. "I'll take you to the mud bogs at Lake Abundance. Then we'll see who's the little old lady."

He laughed. "I'll bring a video camera. Just in case."

In a strange way, having the Wheatleys around turned out to be a good thing during the next two days. Helping to keep them busy kept me busy. And Amberlee really was helpful with Dad. If she came into the front room and saw him sleeping in a chair, she'd cover him with a blanket. If she saw that he hadn't eaten his lunch or dinner, she'd make him a bowl of soup and sit there talking with him while he ate it. Always managing to do it in such a way that Dad didn't seem to notice that she was paying special attention to him because he was sick, something he'd always hated.

With his news out in the open, Dad had quit working so hard at hiding how poorly he was actually feeling, making me wonder how he'd been able to cover it at all. If he ate, he threw up. If he didn't eat, he threw up. He had an almost constant headache that pain relievers couldn't touch. He was fatigued. Weak. Losing weight.

It occurred to me late Friday afternoon that I hadn't spoken one-on-one with my sister since Dad had told her about his illness. She seemed to be functioning normally enough, maybe even better than what I'd have expected, but I knew she could simply be putting on a strong face for Dad's benefit and because we had clients in the house. I decided to go talk to her. To see how she was really doing.

Not finding her in the kitchen or supply room or in the front room with Dad, I walked quickly up the stairs and approached her bedroom door. It was closed but not all the way.

As I lifted my hand to knock, I heard laughter from the other side of the door.

Two girls. Giggling over a picture, it sounded like from Amberlee's comments. Probably that stupid one of me rolling my ATV over backwards in a mud puddle. Jacy displayed the thing proudly on the wall above her desk. Framed, matted, dated, but not signed thank you very much, though she did ask.

Sure enough, after the laughter quieted, I heard Jacy say, "We had to go pull it off of him before he drowned."

"That must have been scary," Amberlee said.

"He was mad more than anything else." Jacy laughed again. "It was the mud's fault, then the ATV's fault, then Dad's fault because Dad had only suggested Dakota go around when he could have insisted."

"What did your dad say?" Amberlee had to know.

"He just laughed and told Dakota the mud mask would be good for his skin."

That picture was going to have to find its way to the wood-stove. Sooner rather than later too.

I started to turn away. I could talk to Jacy later. When she wasn't so busy laughing at me. But then Amberlee said, "Speaking of skin, your dad's color is getting worse."

"Yeah."

I leaned my forehead against the rough cold wall.

"Are you scared?"

Talk about a stupid question.

But Jacy said, "I don't know, Amberlee. I mean, yeah, I understand that he's really sick and that it could be because of some really bad things. But I also understand that God had all our days in His hand before we were here to live any of them." She stayed quiet a few moments. "I don't know. That just gives me peace, somehow, like He's bigger no matter what happens."

"It would be nice to have a hope like that," Amberlee said. "In something bigger than us."

"It's Someone, Amberlee," my sister said, "and there's no reason you can't know Him too."

I smiled and shook my head. I'd come upstairs to comfort my sister, and she was doing better than I was. And not only that, she'd opened up an opportunity for herself to tell Amberlee Wheatley about Jesus. Even though I had no doubt I'd learn a thing or two by listening to my sister, who never seemed to struggle as much as I did with leading herself or a conversation or another person in the direction of God, I turned and walked slowly back downstairs.

Saturday morning, Dad and I led the Wheatleys over to Cooke City to load up their SUV and trailer and see them off. This time, unlike when we'd gone to meet them, I towed the sled. After helping Cullen load their things and tie down all their trailer straps, I shook his hand and told him I was glad he'd come to Back Trails.

"Me too," he said, "except for your wreck."

"As long as we learned something," I said.

"I definitely did."

I rubbed my sore left knee. "Me too."

Amberlee approached us then and pulled me toward her in a quick hug while I stood stiffly, like a flagpole in a wind-wrapped flag. When she unhanded me, she said, "You have our e-mail. Let me know how things work out with your dad."

I nodded. I could do that.

She got in the front passenger seat beside her father and waved at me as their outfit pulled out of the lot.

Dad walked over to stand beside me. "So, uh, what was that all about?"

I shrugged. "Haven't got a clue."

We stood together at the end of the paved road and watched the Wheatleys' trailer until we couldn't see it anymore. Then, as Dad stepped over his snowmobile seat and lowered himself onto it, he just had to ask me if I figured I needed to go see Megan Dassinger for a couple minutes before we headed home.

So I just had to answer by knocking him sideways off his seat into a snowdrift. We wrestled there for a couple minutes, laughing and smearing each other's faces with snow until Dad said he'd had enough, and I believed him and we stopped, lying perfectly still and staring up at the gray white sky, catching our breath.

"Dakota?"

"Yeah, Dad?"

"I made my share of mistakes in this thing. I just want you to know I know that. Man to man."

"Your mistakes didn't cost us thousands of dollars."

"They might have cost us our business."

CHAPTER 18

My math book sat open on my desk in front of me, and my pencil was warm in my fingers from its half hour or more of sitting there, but the paper on which I was theoretically doing my assignment was blank except for the number one that I'd written in the left margin of the top line. It wasn't that I didn't understand the math. I did. On any other day I would have had these thirty problems finished in ten or fifteen minutes. But tonight I couldn't concentrate. And I didn't want to admit it and close my book because then I wouldn't even have the hope or pretense of a potential distraction.

It was Saturday night, and Dad's doctor still hadn't called with his test results. And now the house was empty except for Dad, Jace, and me. Quiet. Anxious.

A gentle knock behind me interrupted my not-getting-my-assignment-done session. I set my pencil down and gratefully pulled open the door.

"Hey," Dad said as he walked by me and made his way to the chair I'd just been sitting in.

"Hey." I shut the door.

"I can't take any more of your sister fussing over me," he said.

I smiled.

"What are you doing?" He gestured toward the open book on my desk.

"Trying to get my math done."

"Don't you mean started?"

We laughed.

"Tell you what," he said. "Let's see which one of us can get these problems done first."

"Like a race?"

"Yeah. Like a race."

"Dad," I said, "if you don't feel—"

"If you start fussing over me too, I'm going to go lock myself in my own room and not answer the door."

I held up my hands. "No fussing."

"Good. Because I just need to do something to get my mind off of how lousy I feel right now."

I positioned the math book so that both of us could see it, sat on the edge of my bed with my notebook and pencil, and said go. Dad won the race, but I did finish my assignment. He also won the game of chess we played after that, but I won at backgammon. Then Dad stretched out on my bed, accepted the quilt I handed to him—one of the ones Mom had made—and fell asleep.

I grabbed one of my other quilts, turned out the light, and headed downstairs to find Jacy. I left my bedroom door open so we'd be able to hear Dad if he needed anything.

"It's times like this I wish we had a TV," my sister said quietly when I sat beside her on the couch to stare at the dark and empty fireplace. We didn't use it during the winter because the woodstove put out much better heat.

"You could always go watch one of those shopping channels live-on-air online," I teased her. "Or the news."

She laughed. "Like I need a Byzantine bracelet or the rest of the world's bad news."

"What do you want a TV for then? To watch cartoons?"

She only shrugged.

I knew exactly why she was wishing we had a TV. A distraction, plain and simple. But distractions didn't fix anything. They just filled time. "We could play a game of—"

The doorbell rang, startling both of us to our feet.

"Who would ride all the way out here at this time of night?" Jacy wondered aloud behind me as the two of us walked toward the front door.

"Whoever it is," I said, "is going to think we live some kind of boring life with every waking body in the house rushing to answer the door."

"Maybe it's Megan," Jacy said, only half teasing me.

It wasn't Megan. It was Pastor Blake. He stood on our deck, his snowmobile parked behind him, with a full backpack in his hands.

"Come in." I stepped back to let him by me and then hurried to shut the door. "It's freezing out there."

"I brought stuff for super nachos," he said, handing the backpack to Jacy. "You two hungry?"

Jacy smiled. "We already ate."

"Well, you're teenagers. Eat again."

Jacy nodded and led Pastor Blake to the kitchen while I hung his coverall, gloves, and hat on one of the hooks by the door.

Pastor Blake explained to us while we fixed the nachos and then ate them that he'd learned to be very creative with food during his days in Bible college. His mother had taught him to prepare a few basic meals so that he'd survive on his own and so that her future daughter-in-law would love her, he said, but he preferred anything that could be made with a minimal number of ingredients and a minimal amount of time spent at the grocery store. Things like nachos.

"No sour cream in town," he apologized as we put the last of the food away when we'd finished. "They're better with sour cream."

"They were great," I assured him. "Thanks."

"It's good to have someone here," Jacy admitted for both of us.

Pastor Blake nodded. "I brought some fly-fishing stuff along too. You guys want to help me tie some flies?"

"Sure." I didn't think that either of us had ever tied flies, but they were meant to attract fish whose brains would bounce around inside a hollow kernel of corn. How convincing would the flies have to be?

Two hours later, I'd completed tying only one fly and not all that successfully either. I was hesitantly reaching for the things I'd need to start a second one when we heard Dad upstairs running from my room to the bathroom across the hall. Jacy stood to go to him, but I grabbed her arm and shook my head. "Leave him be."

After several minutes, he came downstairs, greeted Pastor Blake, and then sat between Jacy and me on the couch.

Pastor Blake started reloading his fly-tying gear—hooks, string, rabbit hair, feathers, scentless glue—into the clear plastic tackle box he'd brought it in. "You know what you look like, Hayden?"

Dad laughed. "Some guy with mysterious liver issues who just lost his supper for the sixteenth time in as many days?"

"Well, that too." The pastor smiled, but only for a second. "You look like someone who's been facing his own mortality."

Dad, Jacy, and I sat there in stunned silence.

Even though Pastor Blake was our local pastor and had been since just a few weeks after Dad had become a Christian, none of us knew him very well. We liked his preaching well enough and appreciated his efforts at balancing the needs of tourists and local church members, but we still called or e-mailed Pastor Adams in Billings with any questions we had about God or the Bible. Dad knew him and trusted him. They had shared some similar life experiences and were friends. Pastor Blake, though, was at least sixteen years younger than Dad and had so far only experienced school. At least that's how Dad looked at it. And since Dad wasn't one to open up easily to new people, and since he was already comfortable with Pastor Adams, there hadn't been much of a reason for him to give Pastor Blake an opportunity to show us what he was really made of.

Until now.

Dad said, "You sure don't beat around the bush, do you?"

Pastor Blake didn't look the slightest bit embarrassed. "I suppose after a little more time in the ministry I'll perfect the art of what I call pastoral correctness and start sandwiching substance between pleasantries and hunting stories. But we all know what's on all of your minds right now, so why not just get to it?"

I thought Dad might tell the young pastor to mind his own business. Or to save his lack of what he called *pastoral correctness* for someone whose biggest crisis was the offensive thing so-and-so had said about him behind his back. Or to leave.

But he said, "It's not that I'm afraid to die. I'm not. To be absent from the body is to be present with Christ is what the Bible promises, and I certainly can't think of anywhere better to be. It's just . . . Jacy and Dakota."

Apparently Dad had concluded that Pastor Blake was made of more than he'd previously given him credit for. Pastorally correct or not.

"I know I'm on the outside looking in here," Pastor Blake said quietly, "and so that makes the truth easier for me to say. But that doesn't make it any less the truth. You've got to have faith that if God is ready to take you home, Hayden, He's also ready to take care of your kids through the process."

Isn't that what Jacy had been trying to tell Amberlee the day before?

"It's just that simple, isn't it?" Dad took tight hold of Jacy's hand inside both of his.

"Simple, maybe," I agreed. "But not easy."

Jacy leaned in closer to Dad. "There are a lot of things about being a Christian that are that way," she said. "Simple but not easy."

"But doable," Pastor Blake said, "when you're looking in the right place."

"I haven't been doing that." Dad looked steadily at Pastor Blake. "I haven't been able to. Or I should say, I haven't taken control of my own thoughts long enough to stop and see God's place in all of this because of everything else I've been seeing instead like a blizzard around me. The business. Jacy and Dakota's educations. Hospital bills. Who'd help the kids take care of things? What are the laws about children under eighteen inheriting a business? Would we have to sell out and move in order to be closer to where I could get treatment?" He lifted one of his hands and circled it back and forth in front of his face. "My wife's death. All of it blocking my view of where I should have been looking all along."

"Snow-blind," I muttered, recalling Cullen Wheatley's description of trying to keep his eye on me during the mini-avalanche my snowmobiling accident had caused.

Neither Dad nor Jacy needed any explanation. And I suspected, now that he'd been here for the full first half of winter, that Pastor Blake didn't need one either.

We'd all experienced *snow-blindness* at one time or another for one reason or another. Getting caught in a sudden whiteout. Wind whipping up drifted snow. A skiing misstep. Rolling a snowmobile. An avalanche.

We should have been looking to God. Not at our circumstances. And especially not at our as-yet uninformed perceptions of those circumstances.

Like Peter when he tried to walk on water, we'd been distracted by the storm howling around us.

Snow-blind.

But not anymore.

Dad was in his office, and Jacy and I were both at the dining room table doing schoolwork when the phone rang late Monday afternoon. Dad answered it and then after a moment called us into his office to listen to whatever the doctor was about to tell him on the speaker phone.

"We've got relatively good news, Hayden," the doctor began, and then went on to explain that Dad's illness was not being caused by cancer or cirrhosis or any autoimmune disorder, but by a rather simple and common hepatitis A virus. Food-borne, most likely. The reason this wasn't determined with Dad's first batch of tests, the doctor explained when Dad interrupted him to ask him about that, was also quite simple. It can take up to three or four weeks for "anti-hep-A-antibodies" to show up in a person's blood work, and during that time there was a window when the blood viral antigen, pieces of replicating viruses, and the blood anti-hep-antibodies, our own antibodies which bond to and neutralize the viral particles, exactly balance each other, preventing a positive test result. "I'm certain your original doctor would have mentioned this window to you at your first visit, Hayden," the Billings doctor said, "so as not to cause undue alarm where there might very probably be a rather benign explanation."

Dad shook his head. He hadn't been told about any window.

In any case, they'd treat his symptoms, he'd take it easy for a couple weeks, and the hepatitis would run its course and go away on its own, especially now that his body had begun making antibodies.

A bunch of fancy medical talk. Medical talk I knew I'd remember for the rest of my life even though I didn't have a clue what half of it meant.

I understood the bottom line well enough.

Dad's predictable future held no more fear or certainty of some life-threatening disease than mine did. He was going to be okay.

"So," Dad said several long seconds after he'd hung up the phone, "who'd have thought I'd feel like celebrating after hearing I've got hepatitis A?"

Jacy laughed as she wiped tears from her eyes and crossed the room to hug him.

"Just knowing that I'm going to feel better eventually makes me feel better now," he said.

"What do you want to do to celebrate?" I asked him after he'd let go of Jacy to give me a hug too.

"How about a snowmobile run?"

Jacy opened her mouth to protest, but I hushed her with a quick warning glance.

"I want to see where you wrecked," Dad said.

When would I learn to see the safety in my sister's instincts? "Are you sure you feel up to that, Dad?" I asked, probably in the exact words Jacy would have used had I not stopped her. "I mean, you are still sick and probably shouldn't overdo it."

Jacy put her hands on her hips and rolled her eyes.

The whole exchange was lost on our father. "I'm going to call Pastor Blake," he said. "Tell him the good news and see if he wants to come up and ride with us."

An hour and a half later, I slowed my snowmobile on an all-too-familiar section of the Goose Lake Jeep Trail and stared across the white meadow at the all-too-familiar slope where I'd crashed Mr. Wheatley's machine.

Dad pulled his snowmobile in beside mine and killed his engine. When Jacy pulled in beside him, he took off his helmet for a long and unobstructed look around. "So this is the place."

It wasn't a question, but I nodded in response anyway.

"Hm." He squinted against the glare of the snow when he pulled off his sunglasses to make sure I could see his eyes and the question in them. "Lots of boulders around here, Dakota. Big ones. I'd have guessed you'd remember something like that without an up-close and personal reminder."

I ran my thumb along the silver handbrake until I felt Dad's gloved hand on my shoulder.

"I'm glad you're okay," he said.

It took two swallows to pull up voice for my words. Words I remembered praying I'd be able to speak. "I'm glad you are too."

Pastor Blake came slowly around the turn and joined us alongside the trail. He switched off his machine and climbed up to stand on its seat to take a better look around.

I smiled. Pastor Adams in Billings would be glad to know that Dad was beginning to spend some time with the young pastor. He'd been telling us all along that we needed nearby input and support if we were going to continue to grow closer to God. And that not only that, Pastor Blake, who'd ended up in quite a challenging kind of pastorate for a new guy, needed the same things from us in order to most effectively serve our church and town.

"Don't hurt yourself up there," Dad teased the younger man.

Pastor Blake jumped from his seat and sank to his knees in the deep snow. "Are we going to go search for what's left of Wheatley's snowmobile?" he asked, looking first at me and then at Dad. He seemed almost eager.

"I'm content to leave it lie until the thaw." Dad slid forward a little on his seat. "Why fight the snow?"

Nodding as if he'd seen more in Dad's comment than the words themselves, Pastor Blake settled himself on his machine again but didn't start the engine. "Hayden, have you thought about advertising Back Trails on some Christian websites?"

Dad shook his head. "I don't advertise anywhere but my own website and in outdoor magazines. And it's not like we need more money or more work to do."

"I'm talking about growing the direction of your business," the pastor said, "not necessarily your number of clients or your financial profit." He started his snowmobile. "Pastors' groups. Couples' retreats. Christian writers' retreats. Winter camps." He backed out onto the trail facing home. "You'd open up your place to a whole new clientele. People who'd be happy to have the outfitting adventure in a God-honoring environment."

"By Christians for Christians," Dad said.

"Exactly."

"As long as you didn't only do that," Jacy said. "Otherwise, who would we tell about Jesus?"

Pastor Blake nodded. "Good point."

"Well, it's stuff to think about and look into while I'm working on getting well." Dad started his machine and pulled into the lead on the trail. "And it's a whole lot more interesting to me than what Wheatley had in mind for the place."

I let Jacy go out ahead of me so she could ride behind Dad and then waved Pastor Blake in behind her. Before following him, I glanced one more time over my shoulder at the place I'd attempted to high mark and slowly along the slope down to where I'd ended up underneath a mound of snow.

Never again.

I gave my machine gas and followed my father, my sister, and my pastor down the Goose Lake Jeep Trail toward home. It seemed that change might still be in the works for Back Trails. But change was not nearly as threatening a thing when a guy could see clearly.